And with that, the three familiars left the underground chamber. Aldwyn looked back as Dalton began closing the cellar doors and caught a glimpse of Jack. In front of Aldwyn, the boy had put on a brave face, but now he appeared overcome with worry. Then the doors slammed shut, and Aldwyn heard the clang of the latch falling into place. Once again, it was down to the familiars to save the queendom from certain ruin—but what if, as Kalstaff had feared, prophecies didn't always come true?

THE FAMILIARS

CIRCLE of HEROES

Adam Jay Epstein
Andrew Jacobson

Art by Greg Call

HARPER

An Imprint of HarperCollinsPublishers

The Familiars #3: Circle of Heroes

Text copyright © 2012 by Adam Jay Epstein and Andrew Jacobson

Illustrations copyright © 2012 by Greg Call

Library of Congress Cataloging-in-Publication Data

Epstein, Adam Jay.

Circle of heroes / Adam Jay Epstein & Andrew Jacobson. — 1st ed.

p. cm. — (The familiars ; #3)

Summary: With Vastia under attack from Paksahara's zombie army, the familiars Aldwyn the cat, Skylar the blue jay, and Gilbert the tree frog must gather seven descendants from the most ancient and powerful animals in the queendom to bring Paksahara down.

ISBN 978-0-06-196116-8

[1. Animals—Fiction. 2. Magic—Fiction. 3. Wizards—Fiction. 4. Zombies—Fiction. 5. Fantasy.] I. Jacobson, Andrew. II. Title.

PZ7.E72514Ci 2012   2012005740

[Fic]—dc23   CIP

                                                                        AC

Typography by Erin Fitzsimmons

17 BVG 10 9 8 7 6

❖

First paperback edition, 2013

For Bernie, Roselle, Phyllis, and Jack, my grandparents.
Whether here or in the Tomorrowlife,
you are my circle of heroes.
—A. J. E.

For Ryder, my son.
You are my greatest adventure.
—A. J.

CONTENTS

1

ESCAPE

Aldwyn cringed from the foul stench gusting in over the eastern wall of Bridgetower. The full moon cast a glow on the macabre parade of approaching zombies, bathing every skull, rib cage, hoof, and paw in a harsh yellow light. Dead animals of all sizes, from great elephants down to swarms of vermin, were ready to attack.

Such a fearsome sight would have caused a lesser familiar to tremble, but Aldwyn's paws remained steady. He stood firm on the Tower Pub rooftop, exchanging glances with his equally stalwart animal companion, Skylar the blue jay. The third member of their heroic trio, Gilbert the tree frog, appeared far less bold.

"Go to your happy place, go to your happy place," Gilbert chanted to keep from panicking. "I'm picturing a bug-infested lily pad."

"An undead army never tires, never grows hungry, and never knows fear," said Skylar, a bit ominously.

"How do you kill something when it's already dead?" asked Aldwyn. His question hung in the air.

"If I still had my magic, I'd blast them back to the Tomorrowlife," said Aldwyn's loyal, Jack.

"Well, thanks to Paksahara's dispeller curse, we don't," said Marianne to her younger brother. "No human does. Not even Queen Loranella."

Aldwyn looked back out at the dead animal army to see a line of skeletal rams bashing their horns against the outer city wall. Decomposing corpses of bears slammed their claws into the battlements, trying to rip open holes large enough to force their way through.

"It won't be long before they reach the glyphstone," said Dalton, the eldest of the three apprentice wizards.

Aldwyn turned his attention from the outer wall. At the center of the city, a large stone pillar covered in runic symbols stood outside Bridgetower's House of Trials, guarded by the queen's soldiers. This pillar was one of Vastia's three glyphstones. These ancient monoliths had the magical power to summon the Shifting Fortress, but a glyphstone alone could not bring the Fortress forth. It needed to be surrounded by seven animals. And not just any animals. Magical animals. Descendants of the seven species that formed the First Phylum.

These were the animals that Aldwyn and his companions were going to search for, and the reason why they had enlisted the help of Grimslade, Vastia's most notorious animal tracker.

Despite the rams' continued charge, the strong stone barrier resisted crumbling, but it did not escape damage entirely: a few small gaps began to form in the wall.

"So long as Paksahara remains hidden away in the Shifting Fortress, she'll continue to command her Dead Army without fear of retaliation," said Dalton. "Skylar, the map."

The blue jay reached a talon into her leather satchel and removed a rolled-up piece of parchment. She set the map down on the rooftop and smoothed it out with her wing.

"We need you to find some animals," Jack told Grimslade.

"A mongoose, golden toad, wolverine, howler monkey, king cobra, bloodhound, and lightmare," said Skylar.

"We know where a few of them are, but most are a mystery to us," said Jack.

Dalton continued, "We already know a howler monkey who lives in Split River and a bloodhound who lingers in the Gloom Hills. But we'll need your help with the other five."

"What's a howler monkey doing in Split River?" asked Grimslade. "Last time I checked, most of them spend their days banging their drums high up in the Forest Under the Trees."

"She's a familiar to one of our mentor's former wizard apprentices," answered Marianne. "They've been protecting Split River for years now."

Aldwyn had heard many stories about Banshee and Galleon from Skylar and Gilbert. He even remembered seeing some of the letters that Galleon had sent to Stone Runlet, bragging about his adventures.

"If we pick up the howler monkey and bloodhound first, I suggest we then head north to the Abyssmal Canyon," said Grimslade. "That's where the mongooses and king cobras reside, deep within the broken crevices of the Kailasa mountains. I've tracked them once before with my Olfax snout. Give me that pen of yours."

The bounty hunter reached for Skylar's satchel and tried to grab Scribius. But before he could tighten his grip, the frightened pen leaped from his hand, glided across the map, and ducked behind Gilbert. Shady, the shadow puppy who had adopted Gilbert as his dad, let out a ferocious bark at Grimslade, his smoky snout and ears peeking out from the tree frog's flower bud backpack.

"It's okay," Gilbert assured Shady and Scribius. "He's with us now."

Scribius cautiously reappeared from behind the frog, before moving over to the map. Following the bounty hunter's instructions, the magic pen then began charting a course from the Gloom Hills to the Abyssmal Canyon.

"After we pick up a mongoose and king cobra in the crevices of Kailasa," continued Grimslade, "we'll let this do the rest."

Grimslade held up a disembodied wolf's nose that was attached to his belt. Aldwyn knew only too well what this was: an Olfax tracking snout, one of the black magic specialties of the cave shamans of Stalagmos, able to sniff out any prey. Grimslade had used this very snout to track Aldwyn through Vastia only a few short weeks ago. How ironic that now it would be used to aid the former alley cat and his companions, rather than hunt them.

"If I may make a suggestion, perhaps we should save the wolverines for last," said Marianne. "They are allied with Paksahara. One won't come without a fight."

"No animal puts up a fight when it's dead," said Grimslade.

"We must not have made ourselves clear," said Dalton. "All of the animals need to be brought in alive."

"That's going to cost you extra!" replied the bounty hunter.

Aldwyn heard a loud crack and looked up from the map to see that the rams had turned the small gaps in the eastern wall into bigger holes. The vanguard of the Dead Army began to squeeze their way through.

"I don't need to look into a puddle to see that this is going to end badly," said Gilbert, whose innate magical talent was seeing the future in pools of water.

Then, from across the city, the Sun Temple's bell started to chime loudly. Aldwyn had heard it ring only peacefully, to announce the rising sun, but now it was clanging madly, sending a warning to the residents of Bridgetower. And the people heeded its call, running for the safety of their shops and houses.

"Come on," said Grimslade. "We should get moving."

Grimslade led their retreat, leaping feetfirst through the hatch on the roof and into the stairwell below. Loyals and familiars followed, and it was just a matter of seconds before they were back in the Tower Pub. Only the most committed ale swillers remained, the type of rogues content to die with drink in hand. Grimslade pulled a coin from the burlap bag he had been paid off with and flicked it onto the table where he had been sitting not long ago.

Two of Queen Loranella's soldiers, who had chaperoned the young wizards and familiars from Bronzhaven, immediately took their places on either side of the group. Grimslade pushed through the pub doors and led them all down a twisty cobblestoned side street toward the major thoroughfare. As they made their way, Aldwyn could hear the sounds of windows being slammed shut and tables scraping across floors to barricade doors.

The group came to the main road: to the west, it led to the House of Trials, where the glyphstone stood; to the east, Bridgetower's entrance gate. The gate was the only official way in or out of the city and certainly the quickest—that is, when there wasn't an army of zombies laying siege to it. "I know another way to get out," Aldwyn said to Jack. "Follow me."

Jack related the message to the others, and Aldwyn took off in the lead. Not for the first time, he was thinking back to his days as an ordinary alley cat and the beginning of his adventure. Then, he'd been running away from Grimslade. Now they were running together, looking to leave the city before Paksahara's zombie army made escape impossible!

From above, a terrifying cackling seemed to be coming closer and closer. Aldwyn glanced up over his shoulder. Two zombie chimpanzees were running along the canopies and tapestries that lined the outdoor markets. Loranella's soldiers stopped and pulled their swords.

"Keep going!" ordered one of them. "We'll fight them off."

The loyals, the familiars, and Grimslade continued to flee. With every step, Aldwyn could feel his father's whisper-shell necklace—which he hadn't taken off since the day he discovered it—brush against his fur. He turned back one last time to see the soldiers fighting valiantly against the vicious zombie chimp attack.

Aldwyn led his companions down a street lined

with shops that sold copper pots, swords, and other metal goods. Candles in glass bowls atop waist-high lampposts had been lit, illuminating the darkness. They ducked down an alleyway filled with piles of junk and stopped so Jack and Marianne could catch their breath.

A skinny rat emerged from one of the piles.

"Oh, no, you don't!" The rat recognized Aldwyn. "Every time you come through this alley, trouble's not far behind." Not a moment later, Grimslade appeared.

"Wh-wh-what's he doing here?" the rat asked in a panic.

"It's not what you think," said Aldwyn, trying to sound reassuring. "He's on our side."

"Grimslade?"

Aldwyn nodded.

"Huh," said the rat. "I never thought I'd see the day."

Just then the alley wall shattered. A zombie bear pushed aside the rubble, oozing green stomach acid from a large hole in its rib cage. The beast looked ready to attack.

"Aldwyn, do me a favor. Find a different alley!"

With that, the rat scurried under a pile of debris, leaving the others to fend off the grizzly soldier of the Dead Army.

Jack grabbed a half-finished sword from the junk and charged at the bear. The lumbering beast quickly knocked him to the ground and raised a bony paw to strike.

Seeing his loyal in danger, Aldwyn responded quickly. He set his sights on the lamppost and telekinetically lifted the glass bowl off its metal stand. It hovered in the air for a moment before he gathered his focus to launch it down the alley and into the bear's open rib cage. When the candle flame made contact with the bear's stomach acid, the zombie exploded. Flecks of fur and flesh sprayed in every direction. Gilbert was covered head to toe in gooey remains.

Shady popped his head out from Gilbert's backpack and licked the zombie slime off the tree frog's arm.

"Shady!" cried Gilbert. "Even I wouldn't eat that."

Aldwyn climbed over the remnants of the alley wall and led the group down a darker street, where homeless driftfolk were lying about, drinking potions straight out of the bottle.

"Maybe we're better off taking our chances with the zombies," said Marianne, only half joking.

"If this cat intends to have us sneak out through the sewer markets, he might want to think again," Grimslade said to Jack. He gestured to an iron door. "They don't open the Undergate until after midnight."

Aldwyn turned to Jack: "Tell him there's a reason he was never able to catch me."

He pushed a rotting bale of hay aside to reveal a secret trapdoor on the street. The familiars got through easily, but the three loyals had a tight squeeze, and Grimslade had to remove his cloak just to get his broad shoulders through. Once they all had dropped into the darkness, Aldwyn and Gilbert looked to Skylar for aid. She quickly summoned an illusionary torch. It burned with a dim but steady flame. Aldwyn realized just how much stronger his companion's talent for summoning illusions had grown since their journey had begun.

Aldwyn's eyes quickly adjusted to the semidarkness. He and his companions had entered a long, stone tunnel with a stream of slow-moving sewer water moving through it. With the black-and-white cat leading, the group ran through the ankle-deep sludge and down the sloping corridor toward a spot where the sewer expanded into a wide underground complex.

The entire chamber had an eerie glow caused by the light of dozens of wax candles flickering against algae-covered walls. Planks tethered together floated in the sewer waters, forming crude bridges that connected the stone islands populated by cave shamans and cloaked merchants. Some vendors refused to heed the Sun Temple bell's warning call, barely audible down below, stubbornly standing their ground, while others urgently packed up their forbidden wares as they prepared to evacuate.

A cave shaman selling large hairy arachnids and smaller needle-legged ones brandished a dagger in his hand when he spotted the familiars and their human companions approaching.

Grimslade stepped forward, showing his hands. "We're just passing through."

The merchant cautiously lowered his weapon,

just as Gilbert came into the light, still covered in bear entrails.

"Zombie frog! Keep away," shouted the spider salesman. He flashed his knife. "My dagger is venom tipped."

The cave shaman threw the poisonous knife at the tree frog. It was just about to stab Gilbert when Aldwyn stopped it short with his telekinesis. The blade dropped into the sludge.

By the time Aldwyn turned back, the shaman had shoved all his merchandise into a burlap sack and pushed off on a small raft.

"The narrow tunnel to the north leads to the outer moat," said Aldwyn.

Suddenly, a scream came from a hooded female merchant packing up her wares. A zombie snake had coiled around her neck. Aldwyn quickly discovered where the snake had come from, as he watched countless more drop from narrow slits in the ceiling above. Whether they landed directly atop merchants or merely beside them, they didn't wait long to attack.

Almost instantly, the sewer market transformed into a battlefield, as the cave shamans began to use their black-market goods to defend themselves. The snakes were pouring in through cracks in the walls as well, while the familiars, their loyals, and Grimslade ran across the floating planks, trying to escape.

Up ahead, Aldwyn spotted one of the cloaked merchants sucking down a vial of yellow liquid. Once the glass beaker was emptied, every hair on the merchant's body stood on end, and sparks crackled from his fingernails.

He grabbed a zombie snake, frying it instantly. He kicked another one, zapping it backward.

"Storm berry juice can have powerful results," said Skylar, "but crippling side effects."

The words had barely escaped her beak when the man's stomach boomed like there was thunder inside him.

"Now that's a storm I don't want to stick around for," said Aldwyn.

"The same thing happens to me when I eat milkweed bugs," said Gilbert.

As the group sprinted for a dock at the entrance to the north tunnel, Dalton slipped on a scum-coated log and fell. Skylar's loyal dragged himself to his knees, but before he could bring himself back to his feet, one of the undead snakes sank its sharp teeth into his calf. A mighty kick from Grimslade's bronze-tipped boot stopped the snake from taking a chunk out of the loyal's stomach as well.

Marianne gave Dalton's arm a tug to pull him up and resume their run past the battling sewer vendors. One of the vendors was throwing deadly contraptions rigged with whirling blades at the bony reptiles, dicing their skulls and vertebrae into marrow.

For the moment, the living seemed to be holding their own against the dead, but as more of Paksahara's army flooded in through the ceiling and walls, Aldwyn knew time was running out.

When they reached the dock, Skylar flew down and began pecking away at the ropes tethering a large boat. Dalton gave her a hand, unfastening the last of the lines as the rest of the party loaded in. Grimslade spun back and fired off a trio of arrows at the skeletal snakes charging toward them.

The wooden vessel took off down the northern tunnel, leaving the carnage caused by the undead behind. Now out of immediate danger, the companions were able to breathe easier, but it was slow going through the sewer tunnel. The thick muck was hard to paddle through and the only source of light was Skylar's illusionary torch, which floated in front of them.

"How long do you think it will be before the beasts topple the first of the glyphstones?" asked Jack.

"The queen's soldiers are brave," answered Dalton, who had torn off a piece of his sleeve and was using it as a tourniquet on his injured leg. "But courage gives little advantage in a battle like this."

Then several glass jars floated out of the darkness. As they bobbed in the water, Aldwyn could see that each had a different spider corked inside. There was little doubt in his mind that they had belonged to the merchant who had paddled off when they first arrived. And Aldwyn suspected the man would not have let his precious arachnids go unless something horrible had befallen him.

Gilbert shot his tongue out over the edge of their skiff and scooped up one of the jars, which held a prickly rose-colored spider.

"Really, Gilbert?" asked Aldwyn.

"What? I could get hungry later," replied the tree frog.

The boat stopped moving as the hull ground up against something hidden in the murk. Despite their attempts to paddle past it, they were unsuccessful: the boat was stuck.

"What is it?" asked Jack.

"There's only one way to find out." Begrudgingly, Grimslade slipped off his jacket, belt, and crossbow.

He swung his legs into the water and found himself standing in muck up to his waist. He used all his might to push the boat free. It started drifting forward again and Grimslade was about to pull himself back in when to everyone's surprise, he was tugged under.

Loyals and familiars were struck speechless. It was impossible to see anything below the murky surface. Suddenly, Grimslade burst through the water, gasping for air. Right behind him was a zombie crocodile bigger than the whole boat, with shreds of Grimslade's cloak in its teeth.

Dalton grabbed the crossbow and pointed it at the zombie, firing a bolt into the rotting reptile's corpse. Unaffected, the crocodile dove back under, pulling Grimslade with him. The stray hunter disappeared again.

Aldwyn bravely stuck his head and paw into the sludge, but it was in vain. There was no sign of Grimslade or the undead creature. Then, just as he was about to come back up for air, Aldwyn heard Grimslade's voice. It was both far away and yet as clear as if Grimslade was speaking right into his ear.

This is not how I'm going to the Tomorrowlife.

Aldwyn darted his head to the left and then to the right, but he couldn't see where the voice was coming from. Then he was pulled back out of the water by Jack.

"There's nothing we can do," said Jack. "Come on."

"We can't just leave him," said Aldwyn.

With a roaring splash, the rotting head of the zombie crocodile emerged once more. It lunged viciously toward them again, taking a bite out of the wooden stern. Dalton, Jack, and Marianne paddled with all their strength through the tunnel and didn't stop until they reached a small opening in the city wall, which took them out of the sewers and into a moat that stretched across the northern side of Bridgetower. Aldwyn looked back into the darkness and was surprised to feel a pang of loss for Grimslade, who had once been his biggest enemy.

Now out of the city, the group came ashore safely on the far side of the moat, near a dense tangle of trees. Dalton grabbed Grimslade's belt and leather pouch in one hand and his crossbow in the other, then climbed out of the boat with

Skylar on his shoulder. The others followed him, running for the cover of the nearby woods.

Once under the tall trees, Aldwyn, Skylar, Gilbert, and their three loyals decided to stop and catch their breath, resting on fallen logs and mossy rocks.

But their short-lived break was interrupted by a thunderous crash. Aldwyn turned toward the source of the noise and watched as the walls of Bridgetower crumbled. Bricks were trampled underfoot as Paksahara's Dead Army flooded into the city.

"There will be no stopping them now," said Dalton.

Aldwyn looked to the town center, where the glyphstone was being guarded, and wondered just how long it would remain standing.

2

BEYOND THE
ALABASTER WALL

"We'll have to avoid the main road," said Dalton, who had flattened Scribius's map out before them and was tracing a path with his finger from Bridgetower to Split River.

Aldwyn could see out of the corner of his eye that Skylar was shaking her head and ruffling her feathers.

"Dalton's right," said Marianne. "We can follow the Ebs all the way. According to Galleon's letters, he and Banshee reside in a place called the

Inn of the Golden Chalice."

Skylar couldn't hold her beak any longer.

"No," she said. "It's too far and too danger-ous. Without magic, you three cannot join us on this mission. Queen Loranella said it herself. She only allowed you to come to Bridgetower with us because you were under the protection of her guards."

"We can take care of ourselves," said Dalton.

"Did you see what happened to those sol-diers?" asked Skylar.

"And Grimslade?" added Aldwyn.

"Are you suggesting we return to Bronzhaven?" asked Dalton.

"No," said Skylar. "You'd never make it that far."

"I can hold my own," Dalton insisted. "Even without magic."

Skylar eyed the blood-soaked tourniquet wrapped around Dalton's calf. Her loyal winced but remained stoic.

"Stone Runlet is less than a half day's trip from here," said Skylar. "You can hide out in Kalstaff's cellar. The alabaster walls will be able to ward off any attackers."

As usual, Skylar's logic was hard to argue with, and eventually Dalton relented. It was decided that the familiars would accompany their loyals back to Stone Runlet. Then the familiars would set off to find the seven descendants of the First Phylum on their own.

The group made its way through the Aridifian Plains. Aldwyn looked up at the night sky and was reminded of the three stars that had danced and twisted above the treetops, prophesizing that three from Stone Runlet would save Vastia from danger. Although at first he had found it impossible to believe that he, a simple alley cat, was supposed to be one of the Three, he had come to accept the prophecy as true and put complete faith in its magical certainty.

As Aldwyn and Jack walked side by side, Aldwyn's tail brushed up against the boy's leg. He always felt secure and easy when he was next to his loyal. There were moments when he was tempted to ask to be lifted into Jack's arms, yearning to be even closer to him, but he knew that he was no longer the one who needed looking after. Their roles had been reversed, and now it was Aldwyn who needed to comfort Jack.

"Don't worry," he told his loyal, who was clearly still shaken from the dangerous escape through Bridgetower's sewers. "Soon this will all be over, and we'll be back to wand flight racing."

"We were getting pretty good at that." A smile played over Jack's face. "If we get a little more practice in, we might even be able to compete on the Warlock Trail."

"If nothing else, a rematch against Gilbert and Marianne," said Aldwyn.

Skylar led them forward, flying above a dry expanse of scorched plains. Thousands of tiny anthills dotted the ground, each spitting out bits of red lava. This was the work of volcano ants, and while Skylar had the luxury of soaring over them, Aldwyn, Gilbert, and the three loyals had to be careful to avoid the scalding rivulets of magma. It was hard not to torch the bottoms of their feet.

They had made it halfway across the burning sands when they saw a flock of winged eyeballs flapping in their direction.

Paksahara's spyballs!

At Skylar's signal, they stopped walking and huddled close, while the blue jay cast an illusion. A thorny bush appeared around them, hiding them from sight. Unexpectedly, the spyballs dove in for a landing. But instead of heading for the bush, they began sucking up volcano ants and kicking up plumes of sand.

The six remained still within the illusion, watching as the eyes feasted on red ants. Aldwyn held his breath. He became so quiet he could hear whispers coming from the shells dangling from his father's necklace. But his attention was quickly diverted when one spyball got within paw's reach of the bush. Aldwyn had never seen one so close before. He stared directly into the winged eyeball's pupil. To his surprise, he could see Paksahara standing in a cold, square room at the very top of the Shifting Fortress. She was pouring a black powder into a summoning horn. A crystal urn that reached from floor to ceiling stood beside her, filled with wisps of different-colored smoke. Aldwyn could see that the traitorous gray hare was chanting something aloud to herself. As long as the Shifting Fortress remained hidden, Paksahara would be undefeatable. Aldwyn knew they couldn't let that happen: they had to bring the seven descendants of the First Phylum together in a circle around one of the glyphstones to summon the Fortress. Only then could they attack the evil hare and strip her of her powers.

Aldwyn turned back to his companions and saw that some of the sand kicked up by the spyballs had gotten into Gilbert's eyes and nose. The tree frog's eyes bulged as he struggled not to sneeze. Aldwyn put a paw up to his friend's mouth, and Skylar threw a wing over his nose. Gilbert's chest puffed up and his eyes watered as they continued to muffle him. Luckily, before Gilbert lost all control, the eyeballs took to the air. Aldwyn and Skylar waited until the winged spies had disappeared over the horizon. As soon as they removed paw and wing, Gilbert let out a thunderous sneeze.

"You know, they say holding back a sneeze can be very dangerous," said Gilbert. "It can make the veins in your head pop."

"You know what else can be very dangerous?"

asked Skylar. "Having Paksahara hunt you down and kill you."

"True," said Gilbert. "I'm just saying that spontaneous brain explosion would not be a fun way to go."

"I saw Paksahara," interrupted Aldwyn.

"What?" asked a panicked Gilbert. "Where?" He spun around on high alert, as if the gray hare might sneak up on him at any moment.

"Through the spyball," said Aldwyn. "She was in the Shifting Fortress, pouring a black powder into a summoning horn."

"She must have been raising more animals from their graves to fight in her army of the dead," said Skylar.

The blue jay dispelled her illusion before turning to the loyals.

"We need to get you to that cellar," she said. "Paksahara's army is growing stronger."

Passing through a field of sweet-smelling berries, Aldwyn knew they were getting close to Stone Runlet. The tiny stream that gave the place its name came into view, and soon afterward, they spotted what had once been Kalstaff's cottage. Aldwyn looked on it with a heavy heart. He'd lived in the old wizard's peaceful home for magical learning and study before it was reduced to rubble during a battle between Kalstaff and Paksahara. On that fateful night, Paksahara had arrived in the guise of Queen Loranella to kidnap the three loyals. Kalstaff tried to stop her, but Paksahara was too powerful, sending him to the Tomorrowlife with a deadly blow.

"When my magic returns, I'm going to rebuild this cottage," said Marianne, choking up.

Dalton took her hand and gave it a comforting squeeze.

"We've got to get you down to the cellar," said Skylar. "We've been lucky so far, but who knows when another flock of spyballs will pass over-head."

They hurried through the tall grass toward the pair of iron doors that marked the entrance to the underground hideaway. The metal cellar hasp was sealed shut from the rusting bond Paksahara had cast during her battle with Kalstaff. Skylar dipped her wing into her satchel and removed some ground glow worm. She sprinkled it on the latch and waited as it ate through the rust.

"We'll make sure the warding spells are still active," said Skylar. "Then the three of us will be on our way."

Jack pulled open the doors and everyone went inside. Nearing the bottom of the stairwell, there was a noticeable drop in temperature, and the creamy orange-and-white-speckled walls became cool to the touch. Jugs of persimmon wine and barrels of dilled apples were stored in neat rows along with pickled corn and radish cider.

"At least we won't go hungry," said Marianne.

"But we might suffocate if Jack can't take a bath," said Dalton, teasing the younger wizard.

Jack smiled good-naturedly, taking the ribbing in stride. Aldwyn thought that Jack might be the youngest now, but in a few years his magic would outshine both Dalton's and Marianne's—assuming human magic returned, of course. Then he'd be the one making the jokes.

Skylar dipped a wing back into her satchel and blew a plume of silver dust into the air, incanting, "Dust of Eckles, knowledge calls, use your gift and search the walls!"

The tiny cloud of particles spread far and wide, covering every inch of the four alabaster walls and the ceiling.

"If there are any cracks in the magic seal that protects this chamber, this will expose them," explained Skylar.

All the walls glowed brightly when the enchanted dust came into contact with them. Even the two iron doors sparkled with the distinct golden hue of wizardly protection. Aldwyn was satisfied that Jack and the other loyals would be safe here, until Gilbert piped up from over by the pickled corn.

"Um, guys," he croaked. "Why is this part of the wall charred black?"

Everyone turned to look, and sure enough, there on one of the four alabaster walls, behind all the glow, they could see the gray outline of an archway.

"It looks like a hidden chamber," said Dalton.

He leaned his shoulder against the wall and pushed open a secret doorway, revealing a second room of equal size built just behind the first. Although the dimensions were identical, the items housed within were anything but. In place of food rations, there were relics from Kalstaff's younger years: not only dusty tomes but chain mail robes scuffed from battle and the twin swords wielded by Kalstaff when the first Dead Army had tried to conquer the land many, many years ago.

A particularly ominous-looking suit of armor was mounted on the wall. Just glancing at it made Aldwyn's fur stand on end. It was the color of bone, and a cool steam emanated from its faceplate, as if something within was still breathing. A smoky diamond was embedded in the forehead of the mask and there were three other indentations: one in each glove and a third in the chest piece, where matching diamonds must have once been placed. Aldwyn was surprised to recognize the helmet. He had seen it before in a whistlegrass vision, while following his father's glowing paw prints in search of the Crown of the Snow Leopard. The vision formed by the enchanted blades of grass was of the original Dead Army Uprising. And the helmet had been worn by one of the dark mages leading the undead, Wyvern or Skull; Aldwyn wasn't sure

which, but either way, he could feel the pull of evil from the accursed armor.

Aldwyn wasn't the only one awed by the hidden treasures of their former teacher. Skylar was slowly flying along the bookshelf, reading each of the titles. Gilbert eyed vials of unlabeled potions, then asked the question Aldwyn had been thinking.

"Why would Kalstaff keep all this stuff a secret?" Gilbert looked around curiously.

"Maybe he was protecting us," said Marianne.

"From what?" asked Gilbert.

That creepy helmet, for starters, Aldwyn thought.

At the far end of the chamber was a writing desk where Aldwyn's eyes were drawn to something dangling over the edge of a jewelry box: a silver anklet embedded with squares of emerald. Only the Noctonati, a secret sect of knowledge seekers to which Skylar also belonged, wore them. These humans and animals believed learning magic and searching for answers to all of life's mysteries was even more important than the laws of the land.

"Skylar, come look at this," called Aldwyn, curious to know what she'd make of it.

The blue jay fluttered over to the desk. When she saw the anklet, her face filled with surprise.

"People said Kalstaff had once been a member of the Noctonati," said Skylar. "I just never believed it."

She took the anklet in her talon and pointed at an inscription: *KGM*.

"Kalstaff's initials," she said. "So it was true."

Beside a nearby bookshelf, Gilbert sat on Marianne's shoulder. She was flipping through one of Kalstaff's handwritten diaries.

"Do you think you should be reading that?" he asked. "It's private."

"Did you know that Kalstaff and Queen Loranella were once romantically involved?" asked Marianne, rapt. "Until the Mountain Alchemist came between them!"

"It really feels wrong to be snooping like this," insisted Gilbert. He paused for a moment, then curiosity got the better of him. "Well, what did the Alchemist do?"

"He stole her away for himself," said Marianne.

"Listen to this," said Dalton, interrupting them. He was reading a different journal. "Here, he writes about taking Galleon on a trip into the dream world. It's one of the final tests of a graduating wizard."

Aldwyn was less interested by the personal revelations in Kalstaff's diaries; his attention kept getting drawn back to the helmet, which was now sending plumes of cold air out through its nostril holes. He watched as a wisp of chilled vapor slithered through the still air and wrapped itself around a book with no title on its binding. A slight

36

gust swept the book open to a spot in the middle. Aldwyn looked at the page in front of him and saw words written on the parchment in a shaky handwriting. Most of the time, Kalstaff had dictated to Scribius when he needed something to be written, but on rare occasions he wrote notes to the young wizards himself. Clearly, it seemed whatever had been recorded here was so personal Scribius hadn't transcribed it.

I have become troubled lately by a great fallacy that many Vastians have taken to be truth: that all prophecies are divine and certain. My studies are beginning to uncover that this may not be the case at all. Take Eradeigh Wallus, the young goose farmer destined to wield Brannfalk's sword against a herd of tunneler dragons. He tried and failed, and all of the northern villages fell to the beasts' mighty horns as a result. And he was not the only one. The Flora Sisters never built the Sapphire Temple. No legendary hymns could be written about the prophesized warriors of Marth, since they never even rode into battle at all. History only seems to remember the prophecies that come true and turns a blind eye to the ones that do not. A warning to those with a destiny of their own: just because it is written in the stars does not make it so. These words will surely cause great worry among all who depend on the fates protecting them. I must think long and hard before choosing to share them.

Another sudden swirl of cold air ruffled the pages, and then the book was closed once again. Aldwyn jumped back. He knew the evil helmet had played a role in his troubling discovery, but there was no denying that the words had been written in Kalstaff's hand. A sickly feeling crept over Aldwyn. Was the prophecy of the Three as false as the ones that Kalstaff had uncovered? His confidence had grown since he had learned that he did in fact possess magic powers, but were he and Gilbert and Skylar really powerful enough to save Vastia? He looked at his friends, wondering if he should share Kalstaff's warning. But why, he thought. What good would it do to fill their heads with doubt?

Through the iron cellar doors, Aldwyn could

hear the unmistakable chirping of dawn crickets announcing the arrival of the morning sun. Even though he needed no reminder, the sound spurred Aldwyn back to the mission at hand.

"Come on," he said to his animal companions. "We should go."

Skylar looked like she was on a shopping spree, filling her satchel with small spell scrolls and rare dried components. Dalton handed her Grimslade's Olfax tracking snout, which he'd detached from the hunter's belt, along with his small leather pouch.

"These aren't going to do us a whole lot of good down here."

Skylar opened up the bounty hunter's bag and peered inside. "It's a Mobius pouch!"

Aldwyn peered inside. Although small from the outside, it was enormous within, big enough to hold gear ten times its size. Aldwyn spotted a noose stick, dispeller chains, and some traps inside, similar to the one that had snared his tail when Grimslade first tried to catch him, back when he was an orphan cat in Bridgetower.

Skylar placed Grimslade's pouch within her

own just as Gilbert beckoned Shady out from his backpack.

"I'd love to take you along, boy," Gilbert told Shady. "But I think Marianne, Dalton, and Jack might need you here, to help keep them safe." Gilbert turned to Marianne. "He's really easy to take care of. You just need to walk him, once around midnight and again a few hours before dawn. And he has to be hand-fed. Grubs are his favorite. But you have to chew them up for him first. Now, bathing him can be a little tricky. You know, maybe I should make a list."

"I think we'll be okay," said Marianne, trying to reassure her familiar with a smile. "Be careful out there."

Jack got down on one knee before Aldwyn.

"I feel like we've been saying good-bye a lot lately," he said.

"When this is all over, you and I are finally going to go on an adventure together," replied Aldwyn.

"Pinky swear?" asked Jack.

"If I had one, absolutely," said Aldwyn, nuzzling up against Jack's leg.

The boy gave him a final pet under the ear. Then Aldwyn headed for the stairwell that led out of the cellar. Dalton climbed to the top step and pushed open the iron doors.

"Send my regards to Galleon and Banshee," he said.

"We will," replied Skylar.

And with that, the three familiars left the underground chamber. Aldwyn looked back as Dalton began closing the cellar doors and caught a glimpse of Jack. In front of Aldwyn, the boy had put on a brave face, but now he appeared overcome with worry. Then the doors slammed shut, and Aldwyn heard the clang of the latch falling into place. Once again, it was down to the familiars to save the queendom from certain ruin—but what if, as Kalstaff had feared, prophecies didn't always come true?

3

THE INN OF THE GOLDEN CHALICE

"We should arrive in Split River by nightfall," said Skylar, who was leading the way across another long and monotonous stretch of the Aridifian Plains.

"Yes, if we journey by foot," replied Aldwyn. "But we've made this trip much faster once before."

"Oh, no," said Gilbert. "There is no way I'm jumping on the back of a moving horse wagon *again*."

"You'll be fine," said Aldwyn. "Besides, this way, we might get there in time for lunch with

Galleon and Banshee."

"Last time, my tongue nearly got ripped out of my mouth. And a frog without a tongue is like a bird without feathers, a cat without whiskers, or a mosquito sundae without slug cream."

Fortunately, early on in their adventures, the trio had made a pact that majority ruled, so Gilbert didn't have much of a choice in the matter. But there were no wagons in sight.

As the Three continued their trek, the clouds suddenly began to churn above them. Aldwyn looked to the west, where the disturbance was coming from. He could make out Bridgetower's tallest spires and just beyond them, a column of gray ash that funneled into the sky.

"What is that?" he asked.

"It's the essence of magic soaring to the Heavens," said Skylar. "The first glyphstone has been destroyed."

Aldwyn felt something in the pit of his stomach: a sense of growing dread.

The familiars soon caught up with a dirt road twisting into the distance, and although there was little traffic on it, they spotted a caravan of mule-drawn wagons, covered in fabric that was beautifully decorated with driftfolk ornaments. It was no surprise driftfolk were on the move in spite of Paksahara's Dead Army. They knew the roads better than anybody else and could easily find escape routes if they were attacked by the zombies roaming the land.

"All right, Gilbert, let's hitch us a ride," said Aldwyn, getting a running start down the hill toward the caravan. "Remember, it's all in the knees."

"A frog getting jumping advice from a cat," said Gilbert. "That's just embarrassing."

The two chased after the wagons as Skylar flapped her wings above them. Aldwyn made it look easy, bounding through the air and landing on the back of the rear wagon. Gilbert wasn't nearly as graceful leaping aboard, tumbling past Aldwyn into a crate of planters.

"Wow, that knee thing really worked," said Gilbert as he was peeling his face up off the floorboards.

A butter newt looked over at the familiars from a nearby bed of fungus.

"Whoa-oh-oh!" exclaimed the butter newt. "A cat, a bird, and a frog?! Am I in the company of *the* Prophesized Three?"

Skylar held her head high.

"Yes, you are," she said proudly.

"Let me shake your paw and webbed hand and wing," said the newt, gushing. "I've heard so much about you. I mean, the Three are famous!"

He flung his hand out toward Gilbert, who was about to give it a shake when he realized his webbed fingers were covered in dirt from the planters. The butter newt gripped them anyway, shaking vigorously.

"I didn't even know if you were real," continued the butter newt. "But here you are. In the flesh." The newt hardly took a breath. "You're going to save Vastia, aren't you?"

"So it has been foretold by the stars," said Skylar.

Just because it is written in the stars does not make it so. Aldwyn almost said it out loud. Yet here this butter newt stood, like so many other Vastians, believing that these familiars—the chosen ones—would rid the land of evil, counting on them because of a prophecy that might not even be true.

"Our caravan was in Bridgetower when the wall crumbled," said the butter newt. "But I fear it's just the first of many cities the zombie hordes will overtake. Even before the glyphstone there fell, many had split off, diving into the Ebs and walking across its bottom until they emerged on the other side."

"They must be heading toward the second glyphstone," said Skylar. "The one among the ruins of the lost city of Jabal Tur."

"Well, I just feel better knowing that the three of you are out here protecting us," said the butter newt. "Do you think I could ask you a favor? I hope it's not too much of an imposition, but would you mind giving me your autographs?" He spun around and whipped his tail directly before the trio. "You can sign right there on my tail. Make it out to Nigel."

"Scribius," called Skylar. "A little help here."

Scribius popped out from Skylar's satchel and glided over to inscribe the three familiars' names on Nigel's tail.

"So, where are you headed?" asked Nigel. "Or is it top secret?"

"Split River," replied Gilbert, who seemed eager to impress his first fan.

"We're going to visit a wizard," added Skylar. "His name is Galleon. Perhaps you've heard of him. He graduated with high wizard ranking and has gone on to be something of a town hero. He vanquished a river dragon with a single strangle spell and dispatched a pack of werewasps with a ring of silver arrows."

"Never heard of him," said Nigel.

"He's staying as a distinguished guest at the Inn of the Golden Chalice," continued Skylar.

"Sounds fancy," said the butter newt.

"Yes, well, for someone of Galleon's esteem, no luxury is too great."

"In that case, the three of you should be staying there, too," said Nigel. "Crowned with jewels and bathed in dewdrops."

Aldwyn just didn't feel right giving this innocent drifter false hope. He politely excused himself and curled up in a comfortable spot on a stack of rugs. The last thing Aldwyn heard before he fell asleep was Nigel saying to Skylar and Gilbert, "Vastia is in good hands. The stars are never wrong about these things."

Aldwyn's eyes opened to find Gilbert's webbed fingers poking him.

"We're here," said the tree frog.

The caravan had pulled to a stop and Aldwyn glanced around to get his bearings. Up ahead a swinging sign read SPLIT RIVER HARBOR with an arrow pointing toward a small bridge. Beyond the bridge stood a town blanketed in thick fog.

"Farewell, destined ones," said Nigel, who remained perched on the bed of fungus.

Aldwyn and Gilbert said their good-byes and hopped off the wagon. Skylar was already flying over the small footbridge leading to the stone-and-mortar walkways of the riverside town.

The familiars headed in the direction of the harbor, taking in their new surroundings. Through the fog, it appeared to Aldwyn that all of Split River was as grimy and dirty as the rat's alley in Bridgetower.

"Clearly the Inn of the Golden Chalice is

nowhere around here." Skylar made no effort to hide her disgust at the unappealing streets. "The inn must be in the wealthy part of town."

As they got farther into the heart of the town, it became evident that Split River didn't get any better. In fact, it looked like the whole harbor had been destroyed. A large sailing vessel was half submerged, its bow buried in the water and its aft sticking up into the sky. The gold paint of the ship's name was flaking off from rot.

"For a ship called *The Happiness*, it doesn't look very happy," observed Gilbert.

"Looks like Paksahara's Dead Army has already been here," said Aldwyn.

A dinghy slid up to the muddy banks and a posse of men stepped ashore. That is, they would have been men but for the fact that they were only three feet tall. Barefoot, scarred, and dressed in dried sharkskin pants and shirts, they looked threatening despite their size.

"Elvin pirates," said Skylar. "Waist-high plunderers of the sea. What they lack in stature they make up for in temper. Forbidden to serve in the Vastian Army due to their inability to meet the height requirement, they took to the open waters, cutting all ties to country, queen, and even each other. Now they'll sink a ship just to see the bubbles."

The disreputable swashbucklers marched from the river's edge, across the street, and into a ramshackle tavern. Above the door dangled a rusty goblet with the words "Inn of the Golden Chalice" carved onto it.

"There must be some mistake," said Skylar once she had read the sign. "Galleon wouldn't be caught dead in such a place."

"I don't think it's a mistake," replied Aldwyn.

As he took his first steps into the Inn of the Golden Chalice, he immediately felt his paws sticking to the cider-stained floor. Aldwyn moved between muddy boots and dirty bare feet and over peanut shells and shards of broken clay. As he glanced up he could see concealed daggers shoved into the undersides of tabletops and playing cards hidden up the sleeves of gambling patrons. With its lunchtime crowd of drunkards, pirates, and otherwise bad folk, this was no place for a wizard, let alone a town hero. And save for a ferret curled up on the bar top and the mice collecting scraps from the floor, it wasn't a place for animals, either.

"I don't see Galleon," said Skylar, flying above the crowd for a look around. "Maybe this isn't the only Inn of the Golden Chalice in Split River. Maybe there's another one."

Aldwyn didn't have time to respond, because the inn's most unladylike barkeep was bashing a fork against a glass. She shouted in a husky voice: "Paksahara may win, and our days may be numbered, but if this is indeed the end, there's no reason not to have a little entertainment first. Please give a warm welcome to our house magician, celebrating three years performing here on the Golden Chalice stage. Galleon the Magnificent!"

"We found him!" exclaimed Gilbert, relief in his voice.

But Aldwyn was wondering why a wizard as skilled and powerful as Galleon was supposed to be would be performing in an establishment as seedy as this one.

Then the purple velvet curtain opened and a young man emerged. Unshaven and with

51

shoulder-length hair, he was wearing a rainbow-colored robe and comically crooked hat. He held a wooden stick with pine needles in the shape of a star glued to the top. Aldwyn thought he looked more like a befuddled court jester than a heroic wizard. He stole a glance at Skylar. Her crushed expression made it clear that this was indeed Kalstaff's former apprentice standing before them.

"Ladies and gentlemen, I am Galleon the Magnificent, conjurer of things unknown." The so-called magician pulled a bouquet of paper flowers from his sleeve. It was a poor sleight of hand even for this drunken crowd. The pirates let out a chorus of boos.

"He must be undercover, posing as the village idiot," said Gilbert to the others. "He's probably trying to root out some vagabonds."

Aldwyn didn't have the heart to tell Gilbert the truth.

"Now, friends," continued Galleon, his voice barely audible above the din of the tavern, "let me introduce you to my wondrous familiar, whose talent will leave you in awe. The faint of heart should sit down. Presenting Edgar, the mind-reading chipmunk!"

An overweight chipmunk emerged from behind the purple curtain, dressed in a robe that matched Galleon's.

"Chipmunk?" Gilbert's bulging eyes grew even wider. "Where's Banshee?"

Galleon leaned down toward Edgar, as if listening to something being whispered in his ear. Then he turned to a burly man sitting in the front row.

"According to Edgar, you, sir, are hungry for another bowl of peanuts."

"It doesn't take a mind reader to tell me that!" bellowed the angry patron.

"On to my next trick," said Galleon. "Who would like to feast their eyes on the floating balls of Astraloch? And if you like what you see, please drop a coin in the mug. Remember, your money won't do you any good once Paksahara has laid waste to all of Vastia." Galleon pulled two crudely painted wooden spheres, one with stars and one with moons, out from beneath his robe. "Edgar, make the balls dance in the air."

Edgar stared at the two spheres, concentrating, and suddenly they began to rise into the air. But it was obvious to everyone in the tavern that they were both dangling from clear strings tied to Galleon's wrists.

"Let's head backstage and wait for Galleon there," said Skylar. "Maybe he can tell us what happened to Banshee. Besides, I can't bear to watch this anymore."

She flapped away, with Aldwyn right behind her. Gilbert reluctantly followed, eyes glued to the stage. The Three darted behind the curtain and found themselves in a broom closet, where they could still hear Galleon trying to amaze the audience.

"Now the balls will float away, perhaps never to be seen again."

The curtain parted slightly and the balls moved through with strings still attached. From the tavern, Aldwyn could hear more boos and hisses.

"Tough crowd," said Gilbert. "I thought that was pretty neat."

Edgar scurried backstage, huffing and puffing.

Naturally, he was surprised to see three animals standing in the closet.

"This is an exclusive dressing room back here," he said. "The only ones allowed are entertainers and kitchen staff."

"We're old acquaintances of Galleon," explained Skylar. "What's happened to him? I know human magic was recently dispelled from the land, but he couldn't have hit rock bottom that fast."

"Ha!" Edgar laughed. "Galleon hasn't had magic in years."

"You're wrong," said Gilbert. "He sent letters, about slaying river dragons and battling sea trolls."

The chipmunk shook his head. "I don't know what tall tales you've been hearing, but Galleon fell on hard times way before Paksahara started causing trouble."

"If you don't mind me asking, where's Banshee?" asked Skylar.

"She left town years ago," said Edgar.

"Without Galleon? Impossible," said Skylar. "A familiar and loyal stay together for life."

"Not this time," said Edgar. "When Galleon first arrived in town, he was coming to replace an elder sorcerer who had protected Split River for half a century. The city was thriving, safe from ravaging monsters and plunderers. But then Galleon fell in love with a girl named Delilah, the daughter of the richest shipping baron on all of the Ebs. Problem was she had already been betrothed to a wizard named Coriander born to a spice fortune. He challenged Galleon to a disenchantment duel, and if you know Galleon, you know that he never backed down from a challenge."

Gilbert and Skylar nodded.

"They fought the battle right here on the banks of the river." Edgar took off his robe and began changing into his next costume. "Hundreds came to watch. Galleon threw everything he had at Coriander, but he never stood a chance. I'm sure black magic had something to do with it. Coriander seemed to have the spellcasting might of three magicians that day, and he had Galleon on his knees when it was over. Galleon's powers were stripped from him and funneled into a glass vial. Coriander wears it on a chain around his neck as a trophy. And to add to the bitter sting of it all, Coriander forced Delilah, Galleon's true love, to marry him. He keeps her trapped on a lavish yacht and Galleon is powerless to save her."

"That's terrible," said Gilbert, his voice sounding even croakier than usual.

"Soon after, Galleon got a job here in exchange for room and board. He performs twice a day and washes dishes and cleans chamber pots in between."

"And Banshee?" asked Skylar.

"They had a fight years ago and she returned to her monkey village," said Edgar. "As for me, winters can get pretty cold around here. When I heard about this gig, I jumped at it."

"Like Grimslade said, the howler monkeys live in the Forest Under the Trees, high up in the canopies," Skylar reminded Aldwyn and Gilbert, her voice filled with concern. "I was hoping we could avoid a trip into those dangerous treetops."

From beyond the velvet divide, a heckler could be heard shouting, "I got an idea. Why don't you make yourself disappear?!"

"Sir, could you at least stand up when you insult

me," Galleon snapped back. "Oh, you *are* standing up."

The next thing Aldwyn knew, a bar stool was flying through the curtain and over his head.

"You might want to head for the exit," advised Edgar. "This could be messy."

The familiars pushed aside the velvet curtain and reemerged into the cider hall. A pint-sized elvin pirate now had Galleon in a headlock.

"Nobody ridicules me without paying dearly for it," squealed the elf as he tried to squeeze the air out of the magician, who was three times his size.

Galleon maneuvered himself out of the elf's stranglehold, but now the short roughneck's accomplice was lunging toward him with a rusty knife in his hand.

Aldwyn used telekinesis to pull the knife from the accomplice's hand and smacked him over the head with it, knocking him out cold. Then he, Gilbert, and Skylar made a run for the front door, dashing by belligerent patrons rising from their seats, all too eager to brawl.

More pirates swarmed in, but the familiars battled past them, bursting out onto the sidewalk. Skylar turned back to the inn one last time. "Galleon had such promise," she said.

4

UP THE SPIRALWOOD

"Do you think they'll write fables about the three of us?" asked Gilbert after they had been traveling in silence for a while. "Ones that will be preserved in the Vastian Historical Archives long after we've entered the Tomorrowlife?"

"I think there will be a whole section there dedicated to us," said Skylar. "Just look at how much has been written about Kalstaff, Loranella, and the Mountain Alchemist."

The Three had been heading due south on a

dirt road that led to the Forest Under the Trees. Like the Kailasa mountains, the Forest was a landmark that was visible from far away. Even from this great distance, Aldwyn could glimpse their destination on the horizon, but the journey would take them the better part of the day, as they were not likely to be able to hitch a ride this way.

"Do you think they'll throw us a parade?" asked Gilbert, still lost in his daydream. "I love parades."

"Don't you think you're both getting a little ahead of yourselves?" said Aldwyn. "I mean, we haven't found even one of the seven descendants yet."

"But we will. It's our destiny," said Skylar.

Aldwyn quietly continued walking.

"Well, it doesn't matter what they do to honor us," said Gilbert, "as long as my family is there to see it."

Aldwyn looked down at his father's necklace. The whisper shells hanging from it held the voices of both Aldwyn's mother and his twin sister, as well as his own. This was all he had left of his family.

"I'm sorry, Aldwyn," said Gilbert. "I didn't mean to—"

"It's okay. I haven't given up hope that my sister is out there somewhere. Of course, finding her is another story. She doesn't even know I exist."

"When this is all over, we'll help you," said Skylar. "Whatever it takes."

They might not have been blood, but Skylar and Gilbert certainly felt like family to Aldwyn.

It was nearing dusk by the time the trio reached the edge of the woodlands. Aldwyn had a fleeting memory of the last time he had walked beneath the emerald shade of these colossus trees; he had been with Jack, not long after they had first met. Together they had peered inside the web of a spider nymph and come face to face with a gundabeast. Aldwyn hoped he would not be seeing either of those unfriendly forest inhabitants again today.

Skylar was flying ahead of Aldwyn and Gilbert, doing reconnaissance.

"Where do we begin?" asked Gilbert, looking

up at the miles of green stretching above them.

"Shhh," Skylar called back to him. "I hear something."

Aldwyn listened closely and then he heard it, too: the distant sound of drumming. *Boom bah bah boom. Boom bah bah boom.* The Three followed the beat, which was very clearly coming from somewhere above them.

Skylar flew over to a large, twisty tree with rough bark.

"Over here," said Skylar. "It's a spiralwood. The way it corkscrews should allow you to walk up it like you'd climb a set of stairs."

Aldwyn dug his claws into the trunk and scampered up a few feet.

"Works for me," he said. "Gilbert?"

Gilbert's suction pads didn't have any trouble pulling him up the bark, either.

"There's a reason they call us tree frogs," he said.

Skylar flew beside them, and the familiars ascended higher and higher, approaching a dense layer of pale green leaves that formed a kind of natural ceiling. They pushed their way through it and found themselves looking up at yet another canopy; it was as if they had reached the second floor of a building. It was brighter here than below, and colorful flowers were straining toward the pinhole shafts of light that pierced the foliage above. Hundreds of white butterflies with green-and-silver wings were flitting about in the gentle breeze.

A colony of day bats emitted high-pitched squeals as they flew right past Aldwyn, Skylar, and Gilbert and began feasting on the fluttering insects, plucking them out of the air and swallowing them whole. It was only a matter of seconds before the butterflies were gone and the fearsome-looking creatures turned their attention to the familiars.

"Guys, I think those butterflies were just the appetizer," said Aldwyn. "And we're the main course."

The day bats circled back toward them. Frantically, Aldwyn and Gilbert climbed the spiralwood, but they didn't stand a chance of making it through the next ceiling of green before becoming bat food.

"Skylar, now would be an excellent time for one of your illusions," said Gilbert urgently.

"They won't be of any use," she replied, with real concern in her voice. "Day bats don't hunt by sight. They use sound to find their prey."

"So what do we do?!" exclaimed Gilbert.

"Lowering your voice might be a good place to start," whispered Aldwyn.

Too late: the bats let out a coordinated hiss and opened their jaws in unison, ready to attack. But suddenly, the leaves above parted and an enormous winged insect plunged toward them. It had the same white body and green-and-silver wing markings as the tiny butterflies—but its size was mind-boggling. The giant moth ate five bats in one bite, then swallowed another three in the next.

Aldwyn and Gilbert breathed a sigh of relief and raced for the next level while the creature continued its assault on the day bats.

"I think they made the mama butterfly angry," said Gilbert.

"If that's the mama, I'd hate to see what the papa looks like," replied Aldwyn.

They burst through the thick layer of branches and emerged to find themselves dwarfed in a land of giant bugs and flowers: gargantuan spiders were weaving webs the size of castles; buffalo beetles, who usually were just a few inches long, stood taller than the large mammals they were named after. Even a dainty ladybug was terrifying when it was the size of a dragon. Now Aldwyn knew what it must have felt like for the fleas living inside his fur.

"Did we just shrink or something?" asked Gilbert.

"No," said Skylar. "It must be the colossus sap." She pointed to a hole in the tree stem, from which a crimson sap was slowly leaking. Aldwyn observed an already oversized ant lapping up droplets of the sticky liquid. After a moment, the ant's legs began to stretch, and its body expanded like a loaf of bread in the oven.

"I thought Kalstaff said you had to add lava spice to make someone grow," said Aldwyn.

"What's true for humans and mammals

obviously isn't the case with insects," said Skylar.

Boom bah bah boom. Boom bah bah boom.

The drumming had been steadily growing louder.

"We must be getting close to the monkey village," said Gilbert.

The three continued their ascent, and Aldwyn could feel his legs getting tired. Walking a mile was draining enough, but moving vertically was downright exhausting.

As the familiars approached the next ceiling of green, Aldwyn was hoping that beyond it they would finally find the home of the howler monkeys. But bursting through the foliage, he found himself staring up at the sky, with a beautiful sunset in progress. The leaves on which they now stood looked and felt like a field of grass, and the clouds above seemed close enough to touch. They had reached the top of the Forest Under the Trees—and there wasn't a single howler monkey in sight. What's more, the sound of drumming had faded completely.

"They must be hiding," said Gilbert, stating the obvious.

Aldwyn looked around, and at first, the surrounding area appeared completely desolate. But then he was able to make out a number of huts that were almost completely camouflaged by the treetops. Skylar had spotted them, too, and flew in their direction. Aldwyn and Gilbert gingerly stepped onto the leafy meadow, which fortunately turned out to be strong enough to support their weight. As they got closer, Aldwyn saw that the huts formed a ring around a giant wooden platform, on which he could see drums, a shrine, and a large barnlike structure. Skylar had already landed on the platform and was looking around.

"Banshee, come out," she called. "I know you're here."

Aldwyn looked at Skylar, wondering if she had lost her mind.

"Um, Skylar," he said. "You do realize that no one is here, right?"

"Clearly you aren't aware of what the howler monkeys' special talent is," she replied. "Invisibility." Then she called again: "Banshee!"

But again there was no answer. Aldwyn began to wonder: If somebody who could turn invisible didn't want to be found, how exactly did one go about finding her? That's when something brushed against his fur, and it didn't feel as if it was the wind.

"They seem harmless enough," said a female voice. A moment later a sandy-brown howler monkey materialized before them. "I'm afraid there's no one who goes by the name of Banshee here," she continued.

Aldwyn felt a sharp tug on his tail, but when he turned, no one was there.

"Simka," said the female howler monkey. "That's not polite."

A young monkey appeared, looking embarrassed from the scolding.

Still more howlers discarded their camouflage and revealed themselves.

"Is there another village in these trees?" Skylar asked the female monkey.

"None inhabited by the howler monkeys," she answered.

"Banshee would have left your village many years ago to become a familiar," said Skylar.

"Many of our kind go off to assist wizards," said the female monkey.

"But this one might have come back," said Skylar.

A knowing look immediately crossed all of the howlers' faces.

One with red fur and bulging eyes walked up to them. "You mean Elbara. Banshee must have been her ground name."

"Do you know where we can find her?" asked Skylar.

"She spends most of her time in the cloudbush, meditating," said the red monkey, pointing to one of the far branches stretching skyward from the platform. The familiars looked up and spotted a lone figure, silhouetted against the sky.

By now close to a hundred howler monkeys had materialized. A few had resumed their drumming, but most were simply watching these strange visitors from below. From the curious looks he was getting, Aldwyn figured that strangers rarely stumbled upon this treetop community, and that the familiars' heroic reputation had not preceded them.

The female howler monkey who seemed to be the leader of the colony directed them to a vine ladder hanging down from a branch. Aldwyn and Gilbert started climbing it, and Skylar soared alongside them. As they ascended the gently sloping limb, the sunset's pinks and purples faded, and stars began to shine out from the dark blue.

At the top, a female howler monkey sat cross-legged with her eyes closed. She was beating her hands slowly and rhythmically against a fur-covered drum on her lap, almost as if in chorus with the wind. Her coat of black fur was short around her face, revealing her delicate features.

"Banshee," Gilbert blurted out excitedly.

The monkey opened her eyes with a start.

"Gilbert, Skylar, I can't believe it," she said, leaping to her feet and giving them both big hugs with her arms and her tail. "And who's this?" she asked, turning to Aldwyn.

"I'm Aldwyn, Jack's familiar."

"Oh, right, Marianne's kid brother," said Banshee. "Is he old enough to have his own familiar already? I remember when he was just my height." Banshee paused and looked around. "Speaking of, where are your loyals anyway? And what are you doing up here?"

"You haven't heard?" asked Skylar.

"Heard what?" replied Banshee. "I live thousands of feet up in the air. Not a lot of news reaches me these days."

"There's much that you've missed," said Skylar. "Vastia is in terrible danger. A new Dead Army walks the land and we need you to join us to save the queendom. We have to collect a member from each of—"

"Yes," said Banshee.

"—the seven descendants . . . Did you already say yes?" asked Skylar.

"Uh-huh. Count me in."

"Don't you want to hear what this is all about first?" asked Skylar.

"Doesn't matter," said Banshee. "I've been waiting three years for a chance like this to redeem myself. Stuck in these clouds, alone with my shame. Feeling invisible even when I could be seen."

"Is this about Galleon?" asked Gilbert.

"I should have done more. Kalstaff always taught us that it was a familiar's job to help their loyal no matter what. And I just let him walk into that duel. All because of a silly crush."

"Sounds rather romantic to me," said Gilbert.

"Not when you consider what he lost," replied Banshee. "His magic. His manhood. The trust of the people he had sworn to protect." She paused for a moment before adding, "And me."

"What happened between the two of you?" asked Skylar.

"After Galleon lost the disenchantment duel, I suggested we return to Stone Runlet to seek Kalstaff's help. If there was anyone able to retrieve the vial of Galleon's magic, it would be Kalstaff. But Galleon refused. He was too humiliated, and instead sent letters filled with lies. I couldn't allow a wizard with such great potential to just waste it. Harsh words were spoken between us. Galleon disowned me as his familiar. He said he never wanted to see me again. So what was I to do? A familiar is bonded to one loyal for life. I couldn't just head back to the shop in Bridgetower and find a new loyal. That's when I came home." Banshee took a breath and clapped her hands together. "Enough about that. What's this 'save the queendom' business you've come about?"

"You're one of seven descendants that must be gathered around a Vastian glyphstone," said Skylar. "We have to set out immediately for the Gloom Hills."

"Why would you ever want to go to that miserable place?" asked Banshee.

"We must collect a bloodhound," said Skylar.

"Ah." Banshee nodded. "Zabulon's brother, Simeon."

"Yes. We were hoping to make it there before morning."

"I'll have us there within the hour," said Banshee. She strapped her drums to her back and let out a howl that lived up to her species' name. Heeding her call, a gray-and-red moth the size of a river raft flapped out of the barnlike structure below. Within seconds, it was hovering just inches below Banshee and the Three.

"Hop on," said Banshee. "I hope none of you mind flying."

Gilbert's eyes went wider than usual.

"Um, actually, I had a very traumatic experience on the back of a tremor hawk," he said.

But the others were already climbing onto the giant insect, leaving Gilbert little choice.

"This 'majority rules' thing is really not working in my favor." He reluctantly joined them.

"Elbara," called a voice from one of the thatch huts. "Where are you going?"

"The world is in danger, Mother," replied Banshee. "I don't think I'll be back in time for dinner."

Aldwyn could sense the monkey's renewed vigor as she grabbed the long reins that were attached to the moth's head.

"To the Gloom Hills," Banshee howled, giving the reins a firm tug. The giant insect took to the sky, with even Skylar perched atop it for the ride.

It didn't take long for Aldwyn to realize that riding a moth was very different from flying through the air by way of magic wand. He had seen moths bob and weave around candle flames before, and he had found it dizzying to watch them. Now he was hanging on for dear life as the large insect tipped and tossed through the night sky. Gilbert had gone extremely pale in the face. Banshee, meanwhile, was grinning from ear to ear.

The Forest Under the Trees began to fade away behind them until it looked like nothing more than a green mountain in the distance. The familiars were one step closer to gathering the animal descendants needed to form a circle around the glyphstone. But if Banshee was supposed to be the easy one to find, Aldwyn wondered how they would ever manage to collect the rest before it was too late.

5

GLOOM HILLS

As the gigantic moth zigzagged through the darkness, passing birds desperately tried to steer clear of it. Gilbert had his face buried in his hands.

"Just go to one of your happy places," said Aldwyn, trying to comfort him.

"None of my happy places fly above the clouds," replied Gilbert.

Just then they took an unexpected dip, soaring into a haze of fog that prevented them from seeing anything past the tip of the moth's antennae. It had been an exhilarating ride thus far for Aldwyn, but now he was overcome with melancholy. Missing Jack and thinking about his parents and sister, he wondered if he should be on this mission at all.

Turning to his companions for comfort, Aldwyn noticed that they also seemed disheartened. Even Banshee, so exuberant at the beginning of their flight, had lost her joy.

"Can you feel it, too?" Skylar asked Aldwyn.

"Yes, a deep sadness," he replied.

"Try not to let it overwhelm you," she said. "It's the mist of the Gloom Hills."

The moth began spiraling downward, blindly heading for a landing.

"Whoa, girl, whoa!" cried Banshee, pulling up on the reins. But the insect ignored her, spinning downward too quickly. The howler monkey turned to the familiars. "It must be affecting her, too. She's not responding."

The moth was no longer flapping its wings, as if all hope had vanished. Aldwyn dug his claws into the furry patch on the moth's back. The others prepared for a rough landing as well. But it was only seconds before they crashed into the ground.

When the creature made impact, Aldwyn lost his grip, rolling off its back and hitting the dirt with a thud. He could barely bring himself back to his feet; not because of injury, but because his heavy heart was weighing him down like an anchor.

Once he finally dragged himself onto all fours, Aldwyn was unable to see either the insect or his friends through the thick mist.

"Gilbert, Skylar!" he called out weakly.

"Over here," responded Skylar without emotion.

"I'm so depressed," called back Gilbert. "What's happening to me?"

Aldwyn dragged himself in the direction of their voices. He should have been excited when he finally reached his friends, but he didn't feel anything. Gilbert stared ahead sadly.

"I feel worse than the time I almost threw Aldwyn off the Bridge of Betrayal over a backpack full of flies."

"That was a horrible day." Skylar curled up into a feathery ball and tucked her beak into her wing. "Go on without me," she said.

As Aldwyn looked at his sad companions,

he nearly forgot that Banshee was still unaccounted for.

"Banshee," he said. "She's out there somewhere. All alone." Aldwyn dropped to his knees, eyes clouding with tears. "She must be so afraid."

"Don't cry," said the tree frog. "If you cry, I'm going to cry."

Aldwyn began to sob.

And soon the two were both weeping loudly.

Gilbert moved over to Aldwyn and wrapped his webbed arms around him, burying his face in the cat's fur.

Suddenly, Aldwyn felt a surge of relief, as if the sadness was starting to lift and he was becoming himself again.

"Thanks, Aldwyn," said the tree frog. "I feel better."

Just as Gilbert was about to back away from the embrace, Aldwyn reached out and stopped him.

"Wait," he said. "I think the comfort of a friend combats the mists. Hold on to me."

Gilbert planted his hand firmly on Aldwyn's back, and the cat walked over to Skylar. He extended his paw, placing it on Skylar's wing.

He could see the effect of his gesture immediately; she pulled her head out from beneath her wing and looked up.

"See," said Aldwyn. "It's working. As long as we all touch one another, we can make it through here."

"We need to find Banshee," said Skylar.

"Banshee!" shouted Gilbert.

Aldwyn spied the enormous skid mark of where the moth had slid along the ground. He followed its trail, with his tail touching Skylar and the tree frog's webbed hand still clinging to his back, and they found the insect lying limply in the mud. Beside it, Banshee was crumpled up in a heap. The familiars ran over to her.

"Banshee," said Skylar.

Aldwyn got a lump in his throat, unsure if it was from the mists or the possibility that they had already lost their new companion. They gently turned the monkey onto her back and saw that she was still breathing. But the look on her face was so empty that she might as well have been dead.

"Is this the Tomorrowlife?" asked Banshee.

"No," said Skylar, flying over and landing gently on the howler monkey's shoulder.

Banshee cheered up when she felt the friendly contact. Her eyes filled with life once more.

"We must not leave each other's sides," explained Skylar. "Otherwise the mists will fill us with gloom once more."

"Sounds good to me," said Banshee. "And while you're up there, feel free to pick some fleas out of my neck fur."

"I think I'll pass on that," said Skylar.

"So, where do we find this bloodhound?" Banshee asked.

"I'm not sure," said Skylar. "All I know is that Simeon has made the Gloom Hills his home since his loyal died."

The four animals split into two pairs: Skylar and Banshee taking the lead, Aldwyn and Gilbert trailing behind. Leaving the giant moth where it had fallen, the group walked through the dense mists. They came upon three women wearing long brown dresses and veils over their faces, all holding hands and moaning under their breath. The women's sandals dragged across the ground at a somber pace. They didn't even look in the animals' direction; they simply kept walking, disappearing into the haze once more.

"People come here to mourn on the anniversary of a loved one's passage to the Tomorrowlife," explained Skylar. "Some come just for the day. Others stay a week. And many never leave. They remain on the hilltops, listening to the voices of the deceased, hoping to catch a glimpse of their spirits."

They followed the sound of the three women, getting lost in the mist. Soon, Gilbert hopped over to a stagnant stream at the base of a slowly rolling hill, pulling Aldwyn behind him. He dipped his face in to take a drink. After a swallow he spit most of it out.

"Ech, it's salty," he said, wincing.

"It's said that the stream that circles the Gloom Hills is made of tears," replied Skylar. "Tears of the living and the dead that have rolled down the hill and settled here."

"Couldn't you have told me that thirty seconds ago?" asked Gilbert, wiping off his tongue.

Skylar and Banshee continued ahead. Gilbert

just stood there, his feet still ankle-deep in the water. His webbed fingers tugged Aldwyn, keeping him from continuing on.

"If you're thinking about a bath, I wouldn't recommend that, either," said Aldwyn.

"Nuh-uh," said Gilbert. "I see something."

Aldwyn immediately understood what this meant: Gilbert was having a puddle viewing, conjuring a vision of the past, present, or future in the pool of tears.

"Is that Skylar?" asked Aldwyn, glancing down at his vision.

And indeed, the image that had appeared before Gilbert was unmistakable in this calm water. It showed Gilbert frozen in his tracks as his blue jay companion hovered in the air across from him, her eyes staring at him icily.

"She looks even more annoyed with me than usual," said Gilbert.

"*Astula Yajmada!*" incanted the blue jay.

With a mighty flap, Skylar touched her wing tips—one blue, one singed black—together, and a crimson spear materialized. It shot forward and impaled Gilbert straight through the chest.

Gilbert—the one looking at this vision—
jumped back in horror as his likeness in the puddle
collapsed to the ground.

"Ahhhhhhhh!" screamed both Gilberts.

Then the image in the water swirled away.

"Tell me you didn't see that," said Gilbert to
Aldwyn.

Aldwyn stood there quietly for a moment.

"Um . . . which part?"

"It's not possible," said Gilbert. "It can't be possible. Skylar is going to kill me?"

"Gilbert, let's not overreact here," said Aldwyn.

"It's just a puddle viewing."

"*Just* a puddle viewing? Easy for you to say. You're not the one getting murdered by your best friend!"

"Well, you've said yourself that your visions aren't always perfect."

"Not perfect," said Gilbert. "But they always come true. The gray hare who turned out to be Paksahara, the warning in the Time Stream that was sent back to your father—and now this!"

"Hold on," said Aldwyn. "Didn't Skylar say you once had a vision of being attacked by little hippopotamuses, but it turned out they were just floating sour dills in a pickle barrel?"

"That's true," admitted Gilbert after a long pause, but he didn't sound entirely comforted.

"And since when does Skylar cast spears from her wings?" asked Aldwyn. He put a comforting paw on his friend's shoulder.

"Never," said Gilbert.

"And does she have a black feather on her left wing tip?"

"No."

"And do you really think Skylar would ever get

so angry with you that she would *kill* you?"

"Probably not," said Gilbert, still not sounding fully convinced.

"Let's go, you two," called Skylar from up ahead.

Gilbert jumped as soon as he heard her voice.

"Yes, ma'am, coming ma'am," he croaked. "Please don't hurt me."

∽⁘∾

Aldwyn and Gilbert had caught up with Skylar and Banshee. All were now coming up over the first ridge of the Gloom Hills. Through the moonlit haze they could see hundreds of mourners camped along the hillside, some sleeping in the open, others walking in little circles.

A bearded man near Aldwyn was yelling at a rock: "This is my spot. I'm not leaving until my Gertie comes back!"

Aldwyn looked up the slope and could see more figures standing on the hilltops, shouting their grief into the mist. As they continued deeper into the crowd of mourners, Aldwyn began to hear voices, whispers and ramblings. The sounds overlapped one another so he couldn't make out any single one clearly.

"What are they saying?" asked Gilbert.

"That's the curse of the Gloom Hills," said Banshee. "Visitors come here hoping for a message from the Tomorrowlife, but instead all they get is this."

"That explains why so many have gone mad," said Aldwyn.

Skylar approached a potbellied pig sitting quietly nearby.

"We're looking for a bloodhound named Simeon," she said to the hog. There was no response. Skylar spoke louder to get the pig's attention. "Have you seen a dog with brown fur, black paws, long, droopy ears?"

"Everybody's looking for someone here," replied the pig sadly. "How long has he been dead for?"

"He's not," said Skylar.

"Oh, so he's one of us, another mourner," said the pig. "Hm, Simeon, the name doesn't ring a bell. Do you know when he first got here?"

"Years ago, I've been told," said Skylar.

"You'll want to check the crest, then," said the pig, pointing to the hilltop. "That's where the truly crazy reside. The people and animals who have really lost it." His attention was suddenly drawn to an empty area a few feet from where he was sitting. "Now if you'll excuse me, my family is calling. It's dinnertime."

The pig went and sat down by himself.

"Please pass the gruel," he said to no one in particular. Then he seemed to scoop a helping from a plate that existed only in his imagination and began eating it. "Mm, everything tastes delicious."

Aldwyn and the others decided to leave the pig to his heartbreaking delusions. They headed uphill, passing through an ever denser crowd of human and animal mourners.

Suddenly, Aldwyn's head was again filled with whispers and voices, only this time they seemed to be speaking directly to him. To make things worse, he was beginning to think he could see spiritlike figures moving through the mist, too. He saw a black-and-white cat among them. For a moment he was convinced it was Baxley, his father, who had met a cruel death at the hands of Necro, the beast tamer who turned him into glass. Aldwyn broke away from Gilbert's grasp and began chasing the spirit. But just as the ghostly figure got within reach, it disappeared, swallowed up by the mist again.

Then from over Aldwyn's shoulder he heard a recognizable female voice. "Aldwyn," it said. He spun around and looked into the mist, where the spirit of a Maidenmere cat stood. He knew this voice. It was the same one he heard in his whisper shell so many times. It belonged to Corliss, his mother.

"Mom?" asked Aldwyn.

"Your sister . . ." Her voice trailed off.

"My sister? What about her?" called Aldwyn.

The faint voice far in the distance said one word. "Yeardley." Then she was gone.

With Gilbert no longer clutching his tail, the hills were taking full advantage of Aldwyn. His sorrowful feeling was returning, even stronger than before.

Aldwyn turned to Banshee, Gilbert, and Skylar.

"My parents," he said. "They're here. I saw both of them. And my mother, she was trying to tell me something about my sister."

"Yes," Skylar replied. "But the messages from the dead are never complete. That's why none of these mourners leave."

The blue jay might have been right, but Aldwyn felt so close to connecting with the mother and father he never knew, to getting answers about his missing sister—was her name Yeardley?—it was hard to pull away. A pat on the back from Gilbert snapped Aldwyn out of it.

"You okay?" asked the tree frog.

Aldwyn nodded. But his heart felt differently.

The four animals continued their path to the crest, careful to maintain contact the entire way. The higher they ascended, the closer Aldwyn felt he was getting to the Tomorrowlife. With every gentle breeze it seemed as if a spirit passed them by. Aldwyn kept searching, hoping to catch another glimpse of his parents. But instead, he was surprised to see Kalstaff's wise face staring back at him through the mists. The wizard's mouth was moving, as if he was saying something, but the words he spoke were just out of earshot.

"Kalstaff," Aldwyn called out. He had to know: Would the prophecy of the three stars turn out like the others he wrote about in his journal? Were the Three destined to fail? "Will the—"

But before he could finish, Kalstaff was gone.

"The spirits come and go," said Banshee. "It's another cruel trick of the Hills."

"What did you want to know?" Skylar asked Aldwyn.

Aldwyn hesitated, unsure if he should tell her.

"I was just curious if the cellar was safe for our loyals," he lied. "That's all."

Before Skylar could probe any further, Gilbert excitedly nudged Aldwyn: "Look, it's Zabulon," he said.

The others turned to see Kalstaff's familiar barely visible through the mist. Gilbert hopped over to him. Aldwyn was sure that Zabulon would disappear before the tree frog reached him, but he didn't, and Gilbert wrapped his arms around the bloodhound's leg.

Aldwyn, Skylar, and Banshee walked up to them, and Aldwyn noticed that Skylar was looking at Zabulon strangely.

"Gilbert, that's not Zabulon," she said. "It's his brother."

"What are you talking about?" asked Gilbert.

Then he took a closer look and realized his mistake. "Simeon?"

The bloodhound had dark circles under his eyes and unkempt fur.

"Silence," he said. "Nine hundred eighty-one, nine hundred eighty-two, nine hundred eighty-three . . ."

"What are you doing?" asked Skylar.

"Every thousand seconds the voice of my loyal speaks out," replied Simeon distractedly. "Nine hundred eighty-six, nine hundred eighty-seven, nine hundred eighty-eight . . ."

"Are you aware of Paksahara's plot against Vastia?" asked Skylar. "She's raising a new Dead Army of animals to take over the land."

"Nine hundred ninety-three, nine hundred ninety-four, nine hundred ninety-five . . ."

"We need your help," continued Skylar. "In order to defeat Paksahara, we have to collect a descendant from each member of the First Phylum."

"Nine hundred ninety-eight, nine hundred ninety-nine, one thousand," said Simeon.

The bloodhound suddenly stood completely still, listening very intently. To Aldwyn the confusion of voices they were surrounded by sounded like a cacophony of whispers and murmurs, indistinguishable to even the sharpest of ears.

"Follow?" Simeon asked aloud. "Follow what? What are you trying to tell me, Tavaris? Tavaris, speak to me." But no answer came.

The bloodhound lowered his head in frustration.

"One, two, three," he began to count again.

"The voices have a tight grip on him," said Aldwyn.

"I've got an idea," said Banshee, who began unstrapping the drums from her back.

"How clever," said Skylar. "Using the beating sound of your drums to drown out the voices of the dead, so he can regain his sanity?"

"Not quite," said Banshee.

She lifted the drum up behind Simeon and whacked him over the head with it, knocking the bloodhound out cold. Then she grabbed him by the hind paws and started dragging him down the hill.

"Don't just stand there," she said. "Let's see how far away from here we can get him before he wakes up."

⤫

By the time Simeon was coming to, the familiars had already crossed the salty stream.

"Who are you?" he asked dizzily. "And where are you taking me?"

"Away from these hills," answered Banshee.

"But my loyal, Tavaris. He's been trying to tell me something. I have to go back."

"You can't," said Skylar. "You're never going to find the answers you're looking for. Not there."

Simeon looked back at the hill sticking out from the dense mist. A tear fell from his eye and dropped into the stream.

"You're right," he said. "Take me away from this cursed place. And no matter what I say or do, never let me come back."

6

THE OBSIDIAN CLOUD

The Three and their new companions, Banshee and Simeon, had left the mist of the Gloom Hills behind and were heading north. The melancholy that haunted them had disappeared, but in its place, exhaustion had set in. And no wonder: since leaving Bronzhaven two days ago, Aldwyn had caught only two hours of sleep on the wagon ride to Split River. Skylar and Gilbert hadn't even gotten that. All three had been going on adrenaline, but now they started to feel how worn-out they really were.

Skylar brought them all to a stop and laid Scribius's map out flat on the ground. They gathered around her in the moonlight.

"Grimslade suggested traveling to the Abyssmal Canyon next, for the mongoose and king cobra," she said between long yawns that stretched her entire beak open. "Then from there we'll have to figure out where to find a wolverine, a lightmare, and a golden toad."

Simeon's floppy ears perked up.

"If a lightmare is one of the animals you seek, I know where to find the herd," he said. "Many evenings, my loyal, Tavaris, and I would sit together on the banks of the Enaj, looking east to the Yennep Mountains. There we could see what looked like lightning from a storm. Tavaris told me we were seeing sparks flying from the hooves of those majestic horses. It's not far from here, much closer than the Abyssmal Canyon."

"To the Yennep Mountains, then," said Skylar. "Do you know of any shortcuts we could take to get—"

"Zzzzzz!" snored Gilbert, drowning out the rest of her question.

"Gilbert," the blue jay shouted. "Gilbert!"

Gilbert woke with a start, and upon seeing Skylar, his eyes immediately went wide with fear. He jumped behind Aldwyn.

"What are you doing?" asked Skylar.

"Me?" said Gilbert, peeking out from behind his friend. "Nothing. Just had a bad dream."

"You're acting weird," said Skylar.

"Must be the lack of sleep." Gilbert gave a nervous chuckle. Aldwyn knew the real reason for the tree frog's strange behavior, but he couldn't believe Gilbert really thought Skylar would hurt him.

"We're all tired," said Skylar. "But we have to keep moving."

"I can't do it," said Gilbert. "Someone's going to have to carry me."

"Our mission is too urgent. We can't rest," said Skylar. "We are the Prophesized Three. We have to keep going."

"There might be a solution to that problem, as well," said Simeon, who had been noticeably less depressed since the familiars had dragged him from the Gloom Hills. Everyone turned to him. "My loyal was a powerful melder," explained the bloodhound. "Tavaris was crossbreeding different plants, herbs, and spices to make exotic new variants. His Xylem garden was filled with magic components never seen before. He had combined the essence of a morning glory with the bark of a pecan seedling, creating a neveryawn tree whose nuts would give those who ate them a full night's sleep in mere seconds. After Tavaris's untimely death, I tended to his garden briefly before heading to the Gloom Hills. If the tree still grows there, we can collect enough nuts to allow us to make the rest of the journey without sleeping. Best of all, his cottage is on the way to the Yennep Mountains."

He pointed with his paw to a spot on Scribius's map.

The possibility of a full night's sleep, even one that lasted only seconds, was all the convincing Aldwyn and his companions needed.

⁂

Aldwyn didn't remember much of the remainder of the journey to Tavaris's garden. His head felt cloudy, and every time he tried to focus on the task at hand his thoughts would drift back to pillows, blankets, and hammocks and how comfortable each would be right now. Still, his paws managed to walk in step with the others, and he powered through the fatigue.

"Tavaris's cottage is just up ahead," said Simeon. "Past those trees." He quickly used his paw to wipe away what to Aldwyn looked like a tear from his left eye.

"What happened to your loyal?" asked Skylar sympathetically.

Simeon frowned, making his jowls hang even lower than usual.

"A tragic accident. One that I could have prevented."

"I, too, have blamed myself many times for not doing more to help my loyal," said Banshee.

"But you haven't seen how things could have turned out differently, whereas I have," said Simeon. The bloodhound walked ahead, leaving the others behind him.

"What does he mean?" asked Aldwyn.

"It's the magical talent possessed by the bloodhounds from the shores of the Wildecape Sea," said Skylar. "They can walk into the past and witness an alternate path that events could have taken. But they're helpless to change anything."

"So what good is that?" asked Aldwyn.

"That question has been pondered by generations of bloodhounds," replied Skylar. "Zabulon used to say that it allowed him to learn from the past and so make wiser decisions in the present."

The familiars and Banshee followed Simeon past several oak trees with furry orange bark, and it was clear that this was no ordinary cottage garden. The bloodhound led the others past a gnarled hunchback tree with a different kind of leaf on every branch. It appeared as though Tavaris had melded a dozen trees together to form one bizarre monstrosity.

"This is it," Simeon said, pointing a paw at a branch that had feathers instead of leaves. And sure enough, hanging there were clusters of bronze-colored neveryawn nuts, bunched together in threes.

Simeon stood up on his hind legs and grabbed one of the nuts in his teeth, biting it off the tree. He chewed it gingerly and swallowed. Nothing happened. Then Simeon's eyes closed briefly before opening again. Aldwyn saw that the dark circles below the bloodhound's eyes had disappeared.

"Wow, I haven't felt this well rested since I was a pup." Simeon started rolling over in the grass like a younger dog.

Aldwyn reached up next and plucked a nut from the same branch. He cracked the hard outer shell between his teeth, then chewed up the smooth center quickly. It tasted no different from any other nut. But its effect was instant. A wave of muscle-relaxing calm enveloped Aldwyn. He smiled and his eyes began to close. As soon as his lids had shut, they opened again, and Aldwyn felt completely rested.

Skylar and Banshee each ate a nut. Gilbert, however, had trouble breaking the hard shell with his delicate teeth, so Skylar used her beak to crack one open for him. Banshee swung herself into the tree and collected every last cluster of bronze-colored nuts, leaving the branches bare.

"That could keep an army going with no sleep for days," said Simeon.

With renewed energy the group departed Tavaris's cottage and returned to the quest at hand. The farmlands were not far from the calm, green waters of the Enaj River. The animals walked up to the river's edge to get a drink. Gilbert, who had been snacking on salted maggots for much of the journey, lapped up twice his weight in water.

Skylar, Aldwyn, Simeon, and Banshee started quickly upriver, but Gilbert was staring into the water, no longer drinking but watching something.

"Guys, it's Loranella," he called out.

Aldwyn doubled back and looked into the river. Gilbert's puddle vision showed Queen Loranella standing in the garden of the New Palace of Bronzhaven with two of her riders. A courier eagle delivered a rolled-up piece of parchment. Loranella took the message and read it silently to herself, then looked up.

"The glyphstone in Bridgetower has been destroyed," she said to the riders. "And Paksahara's minions have divided. Half are going to join the zombies already marching on the glyphstone of Jabal Tur, and the other half will no doubt be headed here, to Bronzhaven, to destroy the third. Ride to Jabal Tur and warn Urbaugh and the others. Tell them that their most perilous battle is yet to come and they must remain persistent, for we cannot allow another glyphstone to fall. Let us just hope the Three have found the seven descendants."

Both men nodded before galloping off on their horses.

Aldwyn and Gilbert had seen enough of this vision of the present to know that there was not a second to lose. They had to get to the Yennep Mountains and find a lightmare.

The band of five approached the nearest bridge and began to cross the Enaj.

On the opposite bank, several fishermen stood knee-deep in the water, casting their lines in hopes of catching something to eat. As the animals got closer, one of the anglers spat at them.

"If you don't walk on two legs, you can't be trusted," he said.

Banshee looked like she was about to charge him, but Simeon held up his paw.

"Just ignore him," said the bloodhound.

"Yeah, you better keep walking," the fisherman called out. "It's an animal just like you that's responsible for what's happening to these lands. We know all about the queen's rabbit and what she's up to. You all deserve a lot worse than my spittle on your fur!"

Aldwyn noticed that Banshee wasn't the only one who let the man's words get under her skin. Skylar appeared upset as well. She lifted her wing, and Aldwyn watched as a giant shark-toothed eel leaped out from the river, snapping at the fisherman. He stumbled back, falling into the water and soaking himself from head to toe. A satisfied grin crossed Skylar's beak. Her illusions were becoming ever more effortless and never failed to catch their intended targets off guard.

"I forgot what happens when somebody gets on your bad side," said Banshee, coming up beside Skylar.

The animals continued along, the Yennep Mountains firmly in their sights. They crossed a field ravaged by floods, the earth so damp that it was like walking through quickmud. There were small farmhouses sunk into the ground with boarded-up windows; whether residents were holed up inside or had simply abandoned them was impossible to tell.

They hurried on. Near the foothills of the Yennep Mountains the plains became rockier and less fertile. This was a region known as the Chordata Plains, a dry and arid landscape, which made it all the more strange that a flock of swamp storks were huddled nearby.

"You're a little far from the marshlands, aren't you?" asked Skylar.

One of the long-beaked birds lifted its head.

"Paksahara's army has made it unsafe for any animal who refuses to join her. I would rather suffer than stand by her side."

Another stork looked to the animals hopefully.

"We know who you are. We know what you're doing. And we're rooting for you."

Aldwyn and his companions nodded their thanks before continuing on. They headed farther east, fueled not only by the neveryawn nuts but by all those like the displaced storks that were counting on them.

"Guys, would you mind giving me a minute?" said Gilbert. "All that water . . ."

He hopped over to a private spot behind a large rock.

Aldwyn and the others held up for a moment. The wind was blowing in strongly from the north, which, Aldwyn thought, made it quite strange that a solitary black cloud was somehow approaching swiftly from the south.

"It looks like smoke from a fire," said Simeon, who had also noticed the cloud. Particles fell as it passed overhead. Some of the black residue from the cloud stained Skylar's feathers. She lifted her wing to inspect it. "Obsidian," she said. "Paksahara must be sending it forth from the Shifting Fortress to raise more of her Dead Army."

She had barely gotten the words out when Aldwyn felt a rumble nearby, where black specks of the obsidian had burrowed into the ground as if they were worms fleeing the sunlight.

"Gilbert, you might want to wrap things up over there," he called out.

Aldwyn saw the earth open all around them as bones broke through to the surface, coming together like pieces of a puzzle to form the skeletal remains of the great cats—lions, leopards, jaguars, and tigers. Clad in leather and metal armor that was rattling over their bones, they were a terrifying sight. Within seconds, dozens of zombie soldiers were lining up in formation.

"It is Paksahara who raised us," they chanted in unison. "It is Paksahara we follow."

"Now, Gilbert!" shouted Aldwyn.

"Don't rush me," said Gilbert, who was still hidden behind the rock and completely oblivious

to a skeletal jaguar rising up mere feet behind him.

"GILBERT!" screamed Aldwyn. "Run!"

Gilbert finally saw the beast. He let out a croak and sprinted alongside the others just as the jaguar's jaws were about to close around him. "Why didn't anyone tell me we were being attacked by zombies?" he cried.

There was no time to answer. Aldwyn was telekinetically lifting and hurling rocks at the skeletal cats, which were all too quick to attack. Banshee made herself invisible and moments later reappeared on the back of a zombie tiger. The howler monkey swung her drum with tremendous force, knocking the creature's skull around 180 degrees. Unable to see where it was going, the tiger ran straight for a boulder. Banshee leaped off just as the blinded beast made contact with the giant rock and shattered into a thousand pieces.

Aldwyn's eyes scanned for someplace to hide, someplace to escape to, but there was nowhere to go.

"What do we do?" asked Gilbert, glancing over his shoulder in a panic.

The situation seemed hopeless when Aldwyn

heard a sweep of thunderous noise behind him. He looked up to see three white horses running downhill like an avalanche. More followed, leaving a trail of sparks behind them. In unison, the three horses leaped over the familiars, battering through the pack of skeletal cats and trampling a dozen of them underfoot.

A deep, husky voice called out: "Jump on my back!" Aldwyn turned to see that the voice belonged to a tall steed with a silver mane and sparkling black eyes. The lightmare lowered its head, allowing Aldwyn, Gilbert, and Simeon to dash onto its back. Banshee jumped up as well. Skylar soared just above them.

The stallion carrying the animals turned for the mountain and began galloping uphill as effortlessly as if it were crossing flat land. Half a dozen lightmares—for this surely was what these majestic and heroic horses had to be—were holding back the giant cats.

Then a horn blared and one of the skeletal lions called out, "To Jabal Tur."

Upon his command, the zombie soldiers turned to the west and began marching toward the Enaj.

"It was only a matter of time before Paksahara spread her obsidian across the Chordata Plains," said the silver-maned steed. There was no sign of strain in the stallion's voice, even though he was carrying five animals on his back up the rocky slope. Behind them, the other lightmares were galloping in step.

"Who were those cats . . . before they became zombies?" asked Aldwyn. "And why were they all dressed in armor?"

"Prior to their death, they were resistance fighters, great cats who stood up against the oppressive rule of man." He paused. "It's another part of Vastia's forgotten history, one that those on the flatlands know nothing of."

As the lightmare raced along in a flat-out gallop, Aldwyn recalled the pieces of Vastia's forgotten history that he, Skylar, and Gilbert had discovered earlier on their journey. First, there had been the amazing drawings that had been painted on the walls of the Kailasa caves. They showed that before man, animals alone had ruled Vastia. And then there had been the story told to them of how the First Phylum was tricked into allowing a man to join the original council of seven animals. The leader of these conniving humans had been a man named Sivio, who eventually anointed himself king.

"The great cats were massacred on these plains, leaving none to roam the land," continued the steed. "Man tried to cover up the incident by saying that they migrated from Vastia to the Beyond, but in the dead of night their bodies were buried here in the soil of the Chordata Plains."

"More of man's lies," said Skylar, her eyes narrowing coldly. Aldwyn couldn't remember a time she had sounded as angry as this.

"History is filled with them," said the steed. "Which is why the lightmares of Yennep have taken it upon themselves to be the recorders of truth. When Sivio began to cause discord among the original council, our herd was the first to resign. We isolated ourselves up here in the mountains, where we've collected relics of the past and chosen to remain at a distance from the politics of humankind."

As they continued higher and higher up the

trail, Aldwyn noticed that the dusty ground had been hardened into brown stone—no doubt the result of hundreds of years of superheated hooves galloping across it.

Aldwyn turned to Skylar, who still looked visibly upset.

"What is it, Skylar?" asked Aldwyn.

"If we stop Paksahara, who's to say humans won't repeat their past cruelties toward animals?" she replied.

"You can't think like that," said Gilbert. "Not every human is the same. Marianne, Jack, Dalton, Kalstaff, Queen Loranella, Sorceress Edna . . . they're all good people."

"Don't forget what we're fighting for," Banshee added. "For humans and animals to coexist peacefully."

"Peacefully, perhaps," said Skylar. "But not equally. A human has sat on the throne in Bronzhaven for hundreds of years, and never have they sought the advice or counsel of animals. As unpleasant and immoral as her actions may be, Paksahara isn't completely wrong."

The words sent a shiver down Aldwyn's spine.

For Skylar to even think of defending someone as merciless and brutal as the gray hare seemed inexcusable.

"If there's one thing I've learned from walking in the past," said Simeon to Skylar, "it's to think long and hard about the decisions you make in the present. We only get to make them once, and then we have to live with the consequences forever."

Skylar didn't look convinced but made no further comment. Aldwyn could see that they had reached the Yennep Highlands, a long plateau at the top of a mountain. From this elevated position, Aldwyn felt like he was back on the rooftops of Bridgetower, looking down on the entire city, except here all of Vastia could be seen. There was a trail of smoke and destruction across the land, no doubt marking the path of the Dead Army's march.

"These are our stomping grounds," said the stallion as they galloped across a vast alpine meadow, passing hundreds of lightmares who were grazing peacefully.

"Untouched by any outsider," the stallion

continued. "No fences have ever been built. No trees cut down. If the grass is eaten, it will grow back. You are the first to visit, save for the birds, wind, and clouds."

"We are honored to be your guests," said Aldwyn. "We seek the aid of one of your species, a lightmare to join us on our quest to restore peace to all of Vastia."

"You'll need to speak with the tribe's thunderhoof. I'll take you to her now."

They were approaching the far side of the meadow, where a group of white stallions guarded the mouth of a cave. The stallions allowed the steed to walk up to the cavern's entrance and let the familiars and descendants dismount.

Aldwyn was first to enter the cave. It was as long and wide as the grand dining hall in the New Palace of Bronzhaven, but dimly lit. The far reaches were hard to make out from its mouth at first, but as the stallion led them deeper into the mountain, Aldwyn quickly realized just how special this place really was.

The walls were covered in elaborate drawings of animals accomplishing great tasks. The images appeared to have been painted in the same style and perhaps even by the same hand that had decorated the Kailasa cave. Some of the drawings, like those of frogs sitting on thrones and telekinetic cats moving glyphstones, were identical to those at Kailasa. Others were different. One showed the image of woodpeckers carving a bracelet, the same bracelet that allowed Paksahara to control the Shifting Fortress. Another depicted lions, tigers, jaguars, and leopards wearing leather and chain mail armor, marching into battle against man centuries earlier on the Chordata Plains.

There were more recent paintings as well, including one of Kalstaff and Zabulon, Loranella and Paksahara, and the Mountain Alchemist and Edan fighting the first zombie uprising. It was strange to see Paksahara standing alongside Loranella now that she had betrayed her loyal and vowed to rule all of Vastia. One drawing in particular left Aldwyn breathless: in it, a cat, a bird, and a frog were fighting a gray-haired witch and her octopot. It took him a moment to realize that he and Skylar and Gilbert and their battle with Agdaleen had been immortalized here.

"Is that . . . us?" asked Aldwyn.

"Yes," replied Skylar. "We are part of Vastia's history now."

"Are my eyes really that big?" Gilbert asked, wide-eyed.

They continued farther and saw who had painted these magnificent walls, or more accurately, *what* had painted them: magical brushes that dipped themselves into jars of paint made from crushed pollen and vegetable juice, before gliding effortlessly across the smooth rock surface of the cave.

Hundreds of tomes lay open on the ground, with quill pens that looked identical to Scribius writing pages of text. Scribius popped his nib out from Skylar's satchel, then jumped down to the cave floor excitedly.

"I see that you are accompanied by one of the ink dancers," said the steed. "They were created by the lightmares long ago to write down the past in detail, so there would be at least one definitive record of Vastia's history, no matter who attempted to rewrite it. You are lucky to have one among you."

Scribius straightened his tip and held his feather high.

In the back of the cavern, Aldwyn could make out a female horse, her white coat shimmering. She was reading from an old book. The steed stopped before her and bowed.

"Galatea," he said, "I have brought the Prophesized Three, along with two of their companions."

"On stormy nights, the lightmares travel down to the flatlands, when our hooves can go undetected," Galatea said in a voice that was strong and gentle at the same time. "During our last visit, we heard about your calling."

"Then you know how urgent our quest is," said Aldwyn.

"We have remained out of such affairs for many years," said Galatea, "acting as mere observers. But as more pictures have been drawn on the cave walls and history has been recorded in the tomes, I have come to realize that humans and animals can live together peacefully. Lightmares have cut ourselves off from people for too long. We are no longer a part of the history of our land. This needs to be corrected. We will help you to fulfill your quest, and the fastest, strongest, most noble steed of the highlands will join you. There will be a race to determine who among our band is worthy of standing at your side."

Without a further word, Galatea strode toward the exit of the cave. Aldwyn looked to his companions and couldn't help but wonder if any of them were worthy of being on this mission, especially a former alley cat from Bridgetower.

7

THE SCORCH PATH

Aldwyn, Skylar, Gilbert, Banshee, and Simeon stood with Galatea in a far corner of the highlands, where one of the enchanted paintbrushes was drawing a long, red line across the ground.

"So, which horses will be racing?" asked Gilbert.

"Only the very best," replied the thunderhoof.

Galatea blew air through her teeth, letting out a whistle that was loud enough to echo through the morning wind.

About eighty lightmares galloped toward them, each sheer white beast more impressive than the last. All shared the same youthful vibrancy.

"Where are all the elder horses?" asked Skylar.

"They run alongside the young," replied Galatea. "It is hard to tell the difference. I myself am over four hundred years old."

"That's impossible," said Simeon.

"The fields we graze on are filled with life-seed," said Galatea. "It has prevented the horses of Yennep from suffering the ill effects of aging."

Once all of the lightmares had gathered behind the line, Galatea stood before them.

"Lightmares," she said. "As you know, Vastia is in trouble. One from our herd is needed to help these familiars by standing in the circle of heroes that will call forth the Shifting Fortress. Wilhemina, Orion, and Thisby shall run the Scorch Path."

The horses all murmured excitedly.

"The last time that course was raced upon, it led to broken legs and cracked hooves," said a light-mare who limped out from the crowd. "I should know. I've never been the same since."

"I know the Path leaves a toll on those who face it, but the dangers awaiting its victor will be far more severe," replied the thunderhoof. "We must be certain that the one we choose is the most capable of us all."

While the injured stallion seemed no less concerned, he stepped back into line, allowing the proceedings to resume.

"The first to complete the run will represent us on this mission," continued Galatea. "Now, before they begin, each will choose one of the Three to carry on their backs to prove they can keep them safe from danger."

Aldwyn was caught off guard, and by the looks on Skylar's and Gilbert's faces, they were, too.

"Thisby, go ahead."

The lightmare she had addressed, a formidable stallion with small speckles of black on his neck, directed his snout at Gilbert.

"You, little green one, hop on," he said.

Gilbert whimpered nervously.

"I'm much heavier than I look," he said. "And I just ate."

Thisby lowered his head, ignoring him. Gilbert nervously mounted the majestic stallion.

Orion, with coal-gray legs and a proud, rigid

jaw, was next, and he looked at Aldwyn.

"What do you say, cat?" he called. "How would you like to be my squire?"

Aldwyn nodded and pounced onto the lightmare's back, but not before stealing a glance at the injured stallion.

"Don't worry," said Orion. "No harm will befall you. Although I can't promise the same for your long-tongued friend."

"Wait, what?!" Gilbert croaked, having overheard him from the neighboring horse.

"Wilhemina, that leaves you with the bird," said Galatea.

Skylar flitted over and landed atop the leaner, spritely horse's back.

Thisby, Orion, and Wilhemina trotted up to the red line and waited there.

"If you would please send them off with the beating of your drum," Galatea said to Banshee.

As Banshee's hands lifted above her drum, the three lightmares became still, their ears perking up. Each wanted to be the first to take off at the monkey's signal.

Banshee struck the drum.

Bah-boom.

Aldwyn was nearly jolted off Orion's back as the stallion began to run. The three horses sprinted for the edge of the rocky plateau and started galloping down a steep slope. Even though the rocks beneath them were rolling and tumbling under their weight, the lightmares kept their footing.

Aldwyn looked to his left and saw Gilbert holding on to Thisby for dear life with his eyes closed and Skylar perched confidently on Wilhemina's mane. When Aldwyn turned back, he noticed they were heading for a pitch-black tunnel, which they then entered with alarming speed.

The only light came sparking up from the tunnel's stone floor, which was being pounded by the horses' hooves. Wilhemina pulled ahead, but it seemed to Aldwyn as if Orion was holding back. It took him a moment to realize that this was a clever strategy, as the mare was lighting the path ahead. They continued through the narrow tunnel, running up alongside the walls to dodge boulders blocking their way. The only sounds that could be heard besides the thundering hooves were periodic screams from Gilbert.

The sparks that had been guiding Orion suddenly disappeared, and for a moment Aldwyn could no longer see anything. Then he and Orion burst out of the tunnel and into a dimly lit, vast cavern filled by a frozen lake. Wilhemina was already galloping across it. Suddenly Orion sped up and Aldwyn quickly realized why: the heat from Wilhemina's hooves was cracking the ice in front of them. Orion had to leap from one floating island of ice to the next, until he was neck and neck with Wilhemina. Aldwyn heard a splintering sound and spun around to see the frozen lake give way beneath Thisby, sending both stallion and tree frog tumbling into the icy water. Just before Orion sped out of the cavern, Aldwyn spotted a shivering Gilbert pulling himself onto dry land.

It was a short run back into daylight, and Aldwyn was surprised to find that their journey underground had led them far up the mountain. Orion and Wilhemina were now racing across the high peaks of the Yennep. Orion's long strides pulled them into the lead, and the stallion was running straight toward a precipice.

Aldwyn could see that there was another cliff across the chasm, but he was certainly hoping that Orion didn't plan to jump the gorge. Because unless the lightmare sprouted wings, it seemed impossible.

"Hold tight, Whiskers," Orion shouted. "I don't want to lose you."

Aldwyn didn't have time to protest; all he could do was dig in his claws, since Orion wasn't slowing down. The stallion made a running jump, soaring over the forty-foot gap.

Miraculously, Orion landed safely, and a moment later Wilhemina did, too. Orion quickened his pace to a charging sprint as Wilhemina raced past him. She was taking long, leaping strides as she aimed for the red finish line that had come into view. Although Aldwyn knew that it didn't matter whether Wilhemina or Orion joined the familiars on their quest, he was rooting for his own steed to be the victor.

Orion lowered his head and yet again ran faster. If the stallion had been holding back before, he certainly wasn't now. Seeing the red line up ahead, the two lightmares found themselves nose to nose. Aldwyn looked out and saw Banshee and Simeon and a crowd of horses cheering. They stomped in place, creating an earth-rattling welcome to the Scorch Path champion: Orion, who thrust forward, crossing the line first, almost defying the limits of his own legs' speed.

Wilhemina followed just inches behind. She came to a stop, catching her breath. Galatea approached Orion.

"Congratulations," she said. "You have earned the right to represent our band on this quest."

Orion bent down and allowed Aldwyn to hop to the ground. Wilhemina did the same for Skylar, and the two familiars rejoined Banshee and Simeon. Orion stood before the four animals.

"However far this journey takes us, you will have my back to ride upon," he said.

"Not only will Orion carry you and protect you," said Galatea, "but he will act as a traveling historian, too. He'll gather artifacts to chronicle your mission. Future generations of Vastians will never forget you, as earlier ones did our ancestors."

One of the other lightmares trotted up alongside Orion and slipped a saddlebag over his neck.

"I will make sure it is filled with great relics before I return," said Orion. He knelt down. Banshee, Skylar, and Aldwyn climbed atop him, while Simeon remained on the ground.

"These legs might be old, but they'll keep up," said the bloodhound.

"Where are we journeying first?" asked Orion.

"To the Abyssmal Canyon," said Skylar. "Home to the king cobras and mongooses."

"But not without Gilbert," said Aldwyn, suddenly remembering his missing friend.

The words had barely left his mouth when Thisby, covered in icicles, rode up with Gilbert on his back. "I c-c-can't f-f-feel my t-t-toes," said the tree frog, who looked more blue than green. "Could I have a hot cup of tea?"

"Gilbert, since when do you drink tea?" asked Skylar.

"Not to drink," said Gilbert. "To put my feet in."

Banshee reached over, lifted Gilbert off Thisby, and set him down beside his companions on Orion.

"We're ready to go," said Aldwyn, wrapping his tail around Gilbert to help warm up his friend.

Orion didn't need to be told twice. The lightmare took off across the highlands, heading for the mountain trail. The pounding of his hooves against the ground was loud, but it couldn't rival the noisy chattering of Gilbert's teeth right beside Aldwyn's ear.

8

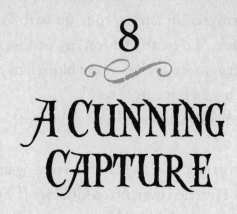

A CUNNING CAPTURE

"*Blue sky, fluffy clouds,
My mind with wandering thoughts,
Of you and loves lost.*"

Gilbert was staring off into the yonder, reciting one of his haikus.

"The frostbite must be making him delusional," Banshee whispered.

"No," said Skylar. "That's just Gilbert."

"Actually, I thought that was one of his better

poems," added Aldwyn. "It didn't contain a single reference to food."

Orion had quickly reached the bottom of the Yennep Mountains and was now racing across the northern portion of the Chordata Plains. Upturned dirt and footprints were the only evidence that hundreds of skeletal great cats had recently risen from the dead here before traveling to the Enaj. Skylar unrolled Scribius's map on Orion's back and studied it as the horse ran. She looked up and pointed her wing due west.

"If we head toward those hills, our path will intersect the Brannfalk Pass," she said, referencing the road named after the long-deceased king of Vastia, Loranella's great-great-grandfather. "From there, we follow it northwest, until we meet the Ebs."

"It is true that your directions would lead us to where we're going," said Orion. "But I know a faster way."

The stallion was already adjusting their course, steering beyond the hills, toward a dense forest.

"Are you sure it's wise to stray from the map?"

asked Skylar, her voice rising an octave, the way it did whenever someone failed to follow her plans.

"You needn't worry, young blue jay," Orion said. "I know these lands better than any map can show. I intend to use that wisdom to give us every advantage I can."

"From here, I defer to you," said Skylar, but her high voice betrayed her true feelings. She rolled up the map and put it back in her satchel.

Aldwyn looked to his fellow travelers: first his two trusted companions, then the three of the seven descendants needed to summon the Shifting Fortress. For the first time since he had read about the failed prophecies in Kalstaff's diary, Aldwyn was feeling confident again. They were quite a team.

Orion reached the edge of the forest and soon they were galloping along a well-trodden path that twisted through trees filled with yellow and red leaves. The lightmare left burning twigs in his wake, his sparking hooves igniting small flames. Without slowing down, he bent his neck to the ground and retrieved a bronze shard of metal from the path with his teeth. Still moving swiftly, he dropped it into the saddlebag slung over his back.

"What was that?" asked Banshee.

"A fragment of a shadow shield," said Orion. "In the time of Brannfalk, those on two legs who profited from trading illegal weapons and components used this road to go undetected by the king's soldiers. It became known as the Smuggler's Trail. Some say this whole forest is enchanted, hiding things that don't wish to be found."

Aldwyn thought he saw fluttering figures out of the corners of his eyes, but every time he turned to look at them, they disappeared. Evidently what Orion had said was true: there were things all around that lurked just beyond their view.

Suddenly, Orion came to a screeching halt, his hooves grinding in the dirt before him. Aldwyn looked down to see what had caused the stallion's unexpected stop. There in the middle of the trail was a small mouse—a small mouse with a horn sticking out from its head.

"Please, help," cried the unimouse. Aldwyn remembered seeing an animal like this in the familiar shop in Bridgetower. "Many have been injured in my village. We had hoped to go unnoticed here among the forest's protective spells, but the hare's minions found us. Wolverine enforcers from Paksahara's animal army came to recruit soldiers from our village. We refused their demands, and we paid dearly for it."

"Did you say wolverine enforcers?" asked Aldwyn.

"Yes," replied the unimouse. "We tried to fend them off with hexes, but our lack of black lichen meant we didn't stand a chance against them."

"When did this happen?" Simeon asked the unimouse.

"Less than an hour ago."

"Do you have any idea where the wolverines were headed next?" asked the bloodhound. Clearly, Simeon had had the same thought as Aldwyn: to intercept the wolverines now and collect the needed descendant from their ranks.

"I'm afraid not," said the unimouse.

"Did they leave anything behind?" asked Aldwyn. "Anything that might give us a clue?"

"I don't know," said the unimouse. "You're welcome to take a look around if you like."

The little creature led Orion off the path, and no more than ten yards away, an entire community of mice appeared before them. Dozens were lying on the ground, some cut and bruised, others with their horns snapped off.

"Aldwyn, see if you can find anything," said Skylar. "Perhaps I can cast some healing spells. I'm no raven, but I'll try my best."

"I'm a bit rusty, but I can try my hand at a few, too," said Banshee.

Skylar and Banshee began their casting and succeeded in closing the unimice's wounds, but unlike a raven, who could reverse any injury, the bird and the monkey could provide merely temporary relief.

A weakened mouse who had lost a horn approached Aldwyn.

"Maybe this will help," she said, holding up her detached horn. On closer inspection Aldwyn could see a tangle of wolverine hair wrapped around the tip.

"Skylar, you should come see this," said Aldwyn.

Banshee continued to tend to the wounded, allowing Skylar to fly over. She examined the tuft of hair, then removed the Olfax tracking snout from her satchel. The disembodied wolf's nose immediately sprang to life, hungrily sniffing the hair. It began to snort and lunge itself toward the south, but was held back by the gold chain it was attached to.

"Looks like they went that way," said Skylar. "We're all thinking the same thing, aren't we?"

"That we should steer clear of these wolverines? Yep," said Gilbert. "They are bad news."

"No, that we go and capture one now," said Skylar.

"Whoa, wait a second," said the tree frog. "I thought we were avoiding them until the very end. Save the worst for last."

"We always knew we'd have to do it sooner or later," said Aldwyn. "We'll use the snout to find them, and once we see what we're up against, we can figure out what to do."

"What happened to going to the Abyssmal Canyon?" asked Gilbert. "Rounding up a mongoose and a king cobra. Two descendants for the price of one."

But the others ignored him, and before Gilbert

could complain about the unfairness of the majority rule yet again, Banshee, who had done what
she could to help the injured, rejoined the group.
The unimouse who had sought their help stood
before them.

"You are the Prophesized Three," he said to
Aldwyn, Skylar, and Gilbert. "Go. Stop that
wretched villain Paksahara before it's too late."

The familiars climbed onto Orion's back with
Banshee. Simeon led the way and off they went.
The lightmare hadn't taken more than a few steps
before Aldwyn turned to wave farewell to the unimouse village—but it had disappeared in a flurry
of leaves, hidden by the forest once more.

Now, as they charged ahead, Orion was not the
only one leading the familiars forward. So, too,
was the Olfax tracking snout.

The animals had entered a darker, thornier
region where the trees had grown so close that
it was difficult for Orion to travel between them.
The stallion was moving stealthily now through
the midday shadows, no longer thundering
across the ground but stepping lightly so as not

139

to tip off the supersensed wolverines they were hunting. The snout was sniffing frantically; if it had still been attached to a face with a mouth, it surely would have been growling. They had to be close.

Orion came to a stop and Banshee, who had volunteered to spy ahead, jumped to the ground. She coated herself in forest berries and crushed leaves to hide her scent from the wolverines. Then she turned herself invisible and disappeared.

Aldwyn and the others waited quietly. Every time Gilbert was about to break the uncomfortable silence, Skylar lifted a feather to his lips. Just a few minutes passed, but it felt like an hour, before Banshee reappeared. Aldwyn hadn't even heard a rustling in the trees.

"There are five of them, just over that wooded ridge," said the howler monkey. "The one who appears to be their leader is skinnier and leaner than the rest."

Aldwyn, Skylar, and Gilbert looked at one another. They all knew who that description matched: Lothar, the leader of the wolverine enforcers. They had encountered him at the Nearhurst

Aviary. Like with the unimice, the wolverine enforcers had been trying to recruit Skylar's family and the other illusion-casting birds of the Aviary into Paksahara's army. With a shiver, Aldwyn recalled Lothar's bloodstained teeth and the double hex branded into the bottom of his paw.

"Do you think you could take them?" Banshee asked Orion.

"With your help, absolutely," answered the lightmare. "But I can't promise that there won't be injuries, or maybe even casualties."

"I'm okay with a few of the wolverines getting hurt or worse," said Gilbert.

"I was talking about us," said Orion.

"Like I was saying, we can still head straight for the Abyssmal Canyon," said Gilbert.

Skylar seemed lost in thought before her eyes lit up. Aldwyn took a relieved breath, knowing the blue jay had come up with a plan. After she explained the details, everyone agreed that it was their best chance at a successful kidnapping.

With no time to waste, the group split up, and Aldwyn moved to the wooded ridge to serve as a lookout. From there he could see the wolverines gathered down below, feasting on the carcass of a no-longer-identifiable animal. Two were fighting over a leg bone.

"Hey, that's mine," Aldwyn could hear one say.

"I brought down the kill," replied the other.

"I'll settle this," snarled a third, all-too-recognizable, voice. Lothar pushed the two other wolverines aside and grabbed the juicy bone for himself.

Just then a stallion made of translucent green energy appeared in the sky, and riding it was a gray hare, who looked unmistakably like Paksahara.

As the flying stallion landed before the wolverines, Lothar dropped the bone from his mouth and bowed down low.

"I did not smell your approach, my gray lord," he said.

"Hiding my whereabouts has become of the utmost importance," replied Paksahara. "Even from you."

Lothar rose back to his feet.

"And to what do we owe this unexpected visit?" he asked. "We have successfully recruited the

High Plains mountain goats and the wall-crawling dingoes. Unfortunately, the unimice chose a different path. Unfortunately for them, at least."

The other wolverines sniggered.

"Well done, Lothar. I knew I could rely on you. Now walk with me—important developments are afoot."

Aldwyn watched as the hare led her trusted enforcer away from his soldiers and into a ravine. He could still see them, and his ears perked up as he tried to catch what was being said.

"We're putting recruitment on hold," said Paksahara. "Your focus now needs to be on killing the Prophesized Three and the descendants they've already gathered."

The hare opened her paw and Aldwyn could see a cat hair, a blue jay's feather, and a tuft of monkey fur.

"I thought I had sensed the presence of these animals in our midst," said Lothar, who seemed to be trying to impress Paksahara.

Out of the corner of his eye, Aldwyn spied Gilbert in a neighboring tree, giving a wave. Then

Aldwyn glanced at Lothar's soldiers, who were still devouring their kill. He used his telekinesis to snap a dry branch and send it crashing into the shrubs on the other side of the pack, far from Lothar and Paksahara. The wolverines immediately jumped to attention, then stalked off to see what had caused the disturbance.

Aldwyn looked over to Lothar, who had also heard the noise. He briefly turned his back to Paksahara to investigate the commotion. But before he had taken as much as a step, an invisible Banshee bashed him across the head with her drum. The wolverine stumbled, but didn't fall. He turned around, but Paksahara and her spectral steed, who of course had been nothing but Skylar's clever illusion, had vanished. For a split second, Lothar was confused—just long enough for Orion to come galloping in, kick up his hind legs, and knock the wolverine senseless.

Skylar soared down from the trees and tossed Grimslade's Mobius pouch to the invisible Banshee. The howler monkey materialized and removed the dispeller chain from the bag. Moving quickly before Lothar came to, she clamped the chain around his neck.

Aldwyn, still on lookout atop the ridge, saw that the other wolverines were returning. He ran down into the ravine, shouting, "They're coming back already. We need to go now."

Orion jostled Lothar awake. "You're going to want to keep up behind me."

The lightmare took one end of the dispeller chain with his teeth. Aldwyn, Skylar, Gilbert, and Banshee leaped onto the horse's back, while Simeon hurried alongside them.

The captured wolverine dug his heels into the dirt to slow Orion's escape.

"Wolverines!" he called out. "I'm being taken!"

Aldwyn turned to see the rest of Lothar's pack burst out from the trees, snarling and drooling. Aldwyn telekinetically lifted four of Grimslade's traps from the open Mobius pouch and flung them into the path of the charging wolverines. Two of the coils missed their targets, but the other two clamped shut around the rabid pursuers' ankles, causing two of them to go tumbling face-first into the ground.

The two wolverines still in pursuit gave an

extra burst of speed, and one lunged forward, biting down on the chain wrapped around Lothar's neck. His fangs shattered on contact, no match for the enchanted steel that had been forged by the cave shamans of Stalagmos. With a loud groan, the beast went somersaulting backward.

Now only one of Lothar's enforcers remained. Orion was racing for a patch of forest dryweed.

"Simeon, sprint ahead," said Orion.

As soon as the lightmare saw the bloodhound was safely away, he rubbed his back hooves together like flint and steel, creating a spark that lit up the dryweed. Lothar was quickly pulled through, but his soldier was not so lucky. Aldwyn looked back and could no longer see any of the wolverines through the wall of smoke and flame, but he could hear them, coughing and wailing in anger at having let these animals escape with their leader.

9

LOTHAR

"**T**his is turning out to be great fun," enthused Banshee. "And here I thought I needed a wizard to go on an incredible quest."

She jumped off Orion's back with vigor and headed over to splash in a stream that was running along beside their path. The other animals joined her to refresh themselves as well.

"I learned a long time ago that animals are quite capable enough on their own," said Orion.

"I, for one, still believe my true calling is and has always been at the side of my loyal," replied Simeon.

"How did you find me?" asked Lothar.

"The unimice told us how you had attacked their village," said Aldwyn.

"So that's how they repay me for letting them live? I should have slaughtered every last one of them. They would have made a nice snack."

"Enough," said Orion. "You should be on our side. Standing beside all those animals who believe in a peaceful future."

Lothar's lip curled, almost as if he was amused.

"It's fitting that you would have me shackled, seeing as how you all fight against Paksahara's stand for animal freedom."

"That is hardly what Paksahara stands for," said Skylar.

"Isn't it, though?" asked Lothar. "All she wants is a Vastia where animals can achieve the greatness that they hold within. Something man has kept from us for far too long."

"And killing innocents is an acceptable means to such an end?" asked Simeon.

"Your humble obedience has left you blind, old dog," replied Lothar. "What do you suggest? Standing by idly for another hundred years of enslavement?"

"You know, man and animal can live peacefully side by side," said Gilbert. "Take our loyals. Marianne and I always help each other out. Or look at Skylar and Dalton. They're like best friends."

"These boys and girls you call *loyals* are the farthest thing from what their name implies," said Lothar. "They use you. You're nothing more than assistants, there to serve them. And if they had to choose between a fellow human and you, I assure you it wouldn't be much of a choice at all."

"You spit out words, but they are little more than hate," interrupted Orion. "You will stand in the circle and do what is needed."

Orion walked Lothar over to the tiny stream.

"Drink. You'll need your strength to keep up with me."

Lothar bent his head down and lapped up a mouthful of water.

Everybody made sure to keep a good distance from him; only Skylar was hovering in the air close by. Thinking himself unobserved, the wolverine, water dripping from his chin, leaned over and whispered to Skylar—but Aldwyn was able to overhear.

"I see the look in your eyes, bird," Lothar said quietly. "Your friends can't see the truth. But you can."

Skylar stared at him for a moment, as if considering his words, before turning away. Aldwyn felt an elbow to his side and saw Gilbert pressing his face up to him.

"Did you see that?" croaked the tree frog. "You don't think she'd turn on us, do you? My puddle viewing. What if it *is* true?"

"Relax, Gilbert," said Aldwyn. "She's on our side."

But as he watched the blue jay fly ahead, he wasn't so sure himself anymore.

⁂

"We should get to the Abyssmal Canyon by nightfall," said Skylar. "And once we collect the mongoose and king cobra, all we'll need is a golden toad to complete our quest."

Sundown was already approaching, and the group was halfway across the Brannfalk Pass, a wide, mud-caked road that snaked toward lush green hills in the distance.

Aldwyn, Gilbert, and Banshee were walking on the ground with Simeon. It felt good. Riding bareback on a horse for hours on end had left them all in need of a good stretch.

Aldwyn looked down to see a grasshopper jumping from one blade of grass to the next. The tiny insect appeared blissfully unaware of the chaos that had engulfed the land. Aldwyn envied its simple existence, a life ignorant of the Dead Army marching across Vastia, free from fear of Paksahara's tyrannical rule. The grasshopper leaped up onto Aldwyn's shoulder; for a moment Aldwyn wished to switch places with it. It would be so easy to live without the pressure of having to save the queendom. To think that this green, long-legged little fellow would spend its days here amid the flower and brush. Blissful afternoons, peaceful nigh—

Slurp.

Gilbert's tongue lashed out and snagged the grasshopper.

"Saltier than I expected," said the tree frog, chewing thoughtfully.

"One's place in the world can change in an instant," said the bloodhound. "One moment you're living free, the next you're lunch."

"Or in my case, one moment you're an alley cat living on the streets, the next you're one of the Prophesized Three."

"I don't hear the confidence in your voice that I would expect from one chosen by the stars." Simeon stared ahead, but Aldwyn felt as if he was looking into his soul.

Aldwyn made sure that Skylar and Gilbert were walking out of earshot before speaking again.

"If I tell you something, do you promise to keep it between the two of us?" he asked.

"Of course," replied Simeon.

"Before we started to collect the seven descendants, I read something in one of Kalstaff's diaries. Something that has called into question everything I believed."

"My brother often told me how wise his loyal was," said Simeon. "What did it say?"

"Not all prophecies come true."

Aldwyn was expecting Simeon to immediately object—to say it wasn't so—but instead a concerned look appeared on the bloodhound's face.

"I haven't told anyone yet," continued Aldwyn. "We need everyone to have faith that all will go well on this mission. To cast doubt would put us all in danger."

"And you really worry that this prophecy may be false?" The bloodhound's voice dropped to almost a whisper.

"When I was chosen by Jack to be his familiar, it was a fluke, an accident. If I hadn't jumped into the store's window at the moment I did, he would have picked someone else."

Then Aldwyn remembered: Simeon was a past walker. He could show him what could have happened instead.

"I need you to take me back," said Aldwyn.

"Sometimes seeing what could have been haunts us more." The bloodhound spoke with caution.

"Please. I have to know."

Simeon hesitated.

I'm afraid you won't find the answers you're looking for.

Simeon said it so quietly that Aldwyn had to do a double take.

"What was that?" asked Aldwyn.

"As you wish," said Simeon.

The bloodhound looked into the distance, and without any further warning, the world around Aldwyn began to change. He felt himself rise half an inch above the ground, then watched as the dirt beneath his feet started turning into cobblestones. Buildings sprouted out from the ground beside him, brick and wooden walls unfolding as easily as paper in the hands of an origami master. The fields surrounding the Brannfalk Pass disappeared, and Aldwyn was back on the streets of Bridgetower, with Simeon as his guide into the past-that-might-have-been.

"You're an impressive foe," a voice called out, "but the chase ends here."

Aldwyn turned to see Grimslade with his crossbow in hand. Across from him was a second Aldwyn, beside a fish pinned to a wooden barrel by an arrow. Another bolt brushed by the second Aldwyn's fur. He made a run for it, dashing around a corner and leaping through an open window.

Simeon and Aldwyn moved through space quickly. Aldwyn didn't even need to take steps yet was still being propelled forward. He phased straight through the wall into the familiar shop, where Jack was standing in front of a cage with Kalstaff and the red-haired shopkeeper behind him.

"I'll take him," Jack blurted out as he stared into the green eyes of the past Aldwyn.

"Are you sure?" asked the shopkeeper. "This is not like a wand or a hat. A familiar must be chosen very carefully."

Jack reached into the cage and pulled the cat out in his arms. The boy stroked the underside of his chin with the backs of his fingers.

"He's sure," said Kalstaff.

Aldwyn watched, yearning for his loyal's touch once more. He turned to Simeon. "I remember all of this. I thought you were going to show me what could have been. Not what was."

Simeon did not respond. He simply nodded, and Aldwyn felt himself getting pulled backward until he was standing in the alley again.

"You're an impressive foe," said Grimslade, "but the chase ends here."

Once again the past Aldwyn was looking at the

fish pinned to the barrel, then at Grimslade. A second bolt brushed by his fur. But this time, instead of running toward the window into the familiar shop, the past Aldwyn snared the fish from the barrel and took off down a different alley. As Grimslade pursued him, Aldwyn and Simeon moved in the opposite direction, through the wall and back into the shop.

This time, the cage where the past Aldwyn would have been was empty, and Jack walked right by it. He stopped and paused for a moment, then doubled back for a second look at a pocket dragon, a scaly snake with wings on its back.

The boy wizard suddenly got a big smile. He put out his arm and the miniature dragon flew onto it.

"I'm Jack."

The snake-like creature shot out a burst of orange flames from its mouth and wrapped its tail around the boy's shoulder. Aldwyn couldn't help but notice how quickly the two gelled as loyal and familiar.

"You and I are going to go on great adventures into the Beyond together," said Jack.

And with that the walls began to bend and twist,

reshaping themselves into the inner walls of the courtyard within the New Palace of Bronzhaven. Aldwyn and Simeon stood watching as Queen Loranella spoke to the young wizards and their familiars.

"We are honored to carry on your legacies," said Dalton.

"That's very noble of you, Dalton," said the queen. "But you, Marianne, and Jack are not the three chosen by the Heavens to protect Vastia." The queen turned to the familiars. "It is you, Skylar, Gilbert, and Karna."

It took Aldwyn a moment to realize that the pocket dragon was standing in the place where he had once held his own head high.

"You are the Prophesized Three," continued Loranella. "The ones that killed Paksahara and brought peace back to the land."

Killed Paksahara? Was it true? Had Skylar and Gilbert, with the help of this pocket dragon named Karna, done what he had been unable to? Did they strike down the gray hare before she unleashed her Dead Army?

If Aldwyn had been having doubts about the

prophecy before, now he was truly troubled: What if the third star that had fallen over Stone Runlet had not been meant for him, but for somebody else? Kalstaff's warning seemed even truer than Aldwyn had first thought.

The Bronzhaven palace walls began to crumble, and all around Aldwyn and Simeon the fields surrounding the Brannfalk Pass returned.

"Aldwyn, if you see any more of those grasshoppers, be sure to let me know," said Gilbert. "I could definitely go for seconds."

Apparently, as far as Gilbert and the others were concerned, Aldwyn and Simeon had never left. After what he had seen, Aldwyn wished with all his heart that he hadn't.

In order to pick up the pace and make it across the pass to the Abyssmal Canyon before it was completely dark, Aldwyn, Gilbert, and Banshee climbed back onto Orion's back. Despite the chain around his neck, Lothar had little trouble keeping pace.

They were making good time, racing past flocks of green sheep grazing in the fields, until the pass descended to the bank of the Ebs. The bridge that had once crossed it here had been destroyed by the river dragons. Their best hope of getting to the other side was by finding the shallowest spot and fording the river on Orion's back. But this came with challenges of its own. Although Simeon could swim alongside them, Lothar would be unable to do so while shackled. A quick vote showed that no one wanted to free him for even the shortest period of time.

"Lift him onto my back," said Orion to Banshee.

"Whoa, wait a second," said Gilbert. "I'm not riding next to that guy."

"We don't have much of a choice," said Aldwyn, eyeing the wolverine, who was giving him a cold, dead stare in return.

Banshee slid off Orion and cautiously approached Lothar.

"Careful, monkey. I bite," he said, flashing his sharp incisors with a snarl of disdain.

Banshee lifted Lothar into her arms and hoisted him up onto Orion. The wolverine's chained legs hung over the horse's sides and his snout lay flat, just inches from Gilbert.

Banshee climbed back on and Orion stepped

into the swift-moving current. No one said a word; only the sound of splashing water interrupted the tense silence. They continued on, and soon the water had risen to Orion's underbelly.

"Have you ever heard the story about the scorpion and the frog?" asked Lothar. "The scorpion comes up to the frog and asks him for safe passage across the river. The frog says, 'Why would I help you? You're a scorpion.' The scorpion responds, 'If I sting you, we'd both drown.' The frog relents, and halfway across the river the scorpion stings him anyway. As they're sinking the frog asks the scorpion why he did it. And the moral of the story . . ."

"It was in his nature," said Aldwyn.

"No," said Lothar. "The moral is that the scorpion was a fool. He should have waited until they got to the other side before killing the frog."

Gilbert shuddered.

"Why does it have to be a frog?" he croaked.

As Orion treaded toward land, Aldwyn wondered if Lothar had made an idle threat or was in fact planning to attack them. All eyes were on the wolverine.

Orion's front hoof touched the western bank of the Ebs. Everyone braced themselves, but Lothar merely let out a nasty laugh.

"Do you think I'd be so stupid as to strike with all of you anticipating it?" asked the wolverine.

Then Lothar bared his fangs and lunged, but his neck went taut an inch away from Aldwyn's nose. Banshee was gripping the wolverine's chains, holding him back.

"Next time you won't be so lucky, cat," said Lothar, his warm breath smelling foul.

Orion stepped completely out of the water and shook it off his body. Simeon emerged not far behind and did the same. Banshee dropped Lothar back to the ground, putting a safe distance between the group and the chained beast once more.

"I will escape," said Lothar. "And your mission will fail. You won't have me, and every other wolverine in Vastia has taken refuge with Paksahara's army. You will have to walk to death's door to find another."

10

STANDOFF AT JABAL TUR

"Look, the queen's soldiers are here," Gilbert said excitedly.

He pointed a webbed finger toward an encampment of gray tents. Pennants staked into the ground surrounded the camp. Each was decorated with the bronze gate that Aldwyn recognized as the symbol of Bronzhaven.

As the group moved closer, they realized that the tents were mostly deserted. A lone fire burned outside one of the larger shelters. Rows of injured warriors were lying on their backs outside the tents, some with severe wounds. A healing raven fluttered from one to the next, rubbing its feathers along the gashes and broken bones. A robed man bandaged them up after the black bird had finished its magic.

The raven recognized Aldwyn, Skylar, and Gilbert instantly.

"The Prophesized Three," said the bird. "You should turn around and get as far away from here as possible. A battle rages between Paksahara's and Loranella's armies for control of the second glyphstone at the center of Jabal Tur. You won't be safe."

"We must get to the Abyssmal Canyon," replied Skylar. "And this is the only way."

They galloped uphill through the trees, the Kailasa mountains looming closer. Occasionally they passed a wounded soldier dragging himself in the direction of the healing raven's tent. Deeper into the pine forest, Aldwyn recoiled from the familiar, unpleasant stench of decaying flesh. He looked to the south and saw a swath of destruction made by Paksahara's zombie hordes. And it wasn't just bony footprints, trampled ground, and crushed saplings that had been left behind. Chunks of rotting muscle and cartilage were scattered like a revolting trail of bread crumbs.

The band of six and Lothar came up over a wooded rise and, in the fading daylight, stared down at the ruins of Jabal Tur. The scene was difficult for Aldwyn to fully take in on first glance. He knew that these ancient ruins had once held a magnificent city, but little remained from that golden time. Marble columns jutted upward, no longer supporting their vaulted rooftops. Patterned tile floors were all that was left of the sun temples. And at the center of the ruins was a giant stone protected on all sides by Loranella's army.

"The second glyphstone," said Banshee, her voice filled with awe.

Dead animals of all kinds were moving in waves against lines of Loranella's shielded and armored human soldiers.

"Look at all these zombies," said Gilbert. "Where did they come from?"

"Paksahara has spread her obsidian all over

Vastia," Orion said. "Some look like they're from the mountains, others the Hinterwoods. I'd bet she's even raised animals from the burial grounds of the once-great zoo of Mukrete."

They could see the first of the Kailasa mountains' many peaks rising behind the battlefield. A narrow crack running all the way down its face marked the entrance to the Abyssmal Canyon. Getting there would be next to impossible given the sea of zombies standing in their way.

"It would be a mighty challenge to trample through the battlefield," Orion said. "I suggest we circle the ruins. It will take longer, but we'll be sure to get there."

No one had a better idea, so there was little debate.

Determined, the group began to move. Suddenly, Lothar screamed out: "Help! Over here!"

Luckily, Lothar's cry went unheard in the clamor of battle. Or at least it seemed to.

Orion had not taken more than twenty steps down the rise when a skeletal gorilla jumped down from one of the trees. The primate's bony forearm knocked Aldwyn, Gilbert, and Banshee clear off the horse's back. Quick to act, Orion delivered a thunderous kick to the undead gorilla's chest, sending the beast backward and a spray of flesh flying just inches over Gilbert's head.

"Phew, that was close," said the tree frog. "Getting splattered with zombie guts once is enough for a lifetime."

Slowed but not stopped by the kick, the gorilla charged Orion again. The lightmare was ready, this time clicking his hooves together and creating a fiery electrical blast that obliterated the skeletal primate on contact. Globs of entrails flew everywhere, covering Gilbert from head to toe.

"Aww, not again!" he cried. "Get it off!"

Banshee was about to help, but before she did, Skylar put up a wing.

"Wait," said the blue jay. "Don't wipe away that slime. In fact, put more of it on."

"Huh?" asked a confused Gilbert.

"And if the rest of you want to make it to the Abyssmal Canyon," continued Skylar, "you'd better do the same."

She moved over to the remains of the zombie gorilla and camouflaged herself in it. Aldwyn walked over next and rolled around in the guts, shuddering as he coated himself in the gooey entrails. The others followed, until the entire group could pass as part of Paksahara's army. Lothar refused to cooperate, but Banshee slathered him anyway.

"Our best hope is to blend in and pretend to be part of the Dead Army while we circle the battlefield," said Skylar. "Once we make it to the glyphstone, our human allies will help us reach the Abyssmal Canyon."

The disguised animals skirted the field, horrified by the power of Paksahara's undead minions.

A commanding zombie coyote shouted orders to his troops. "The glyphstone is vulnerable. Boars, you will serve as decoys. Tigers, attack from the sides." Then the coyote saw Orion. "Stallion, you should be accompanying the main charge against the shield-bearing humans."

Orion pretended to hurry into battle. He was tall enough to see over the zombie soldiers fighting all around them and sent words of reassurance to his companions. "The queen's soldiers are not far now. We'll be safe once we reach them."

Just then a human voice was heard shouting over the roar of battle.

"Charge!"

Ahead, a dozen spear-carrying pikemen ran full speed into the fray, cutting through the surprised zombies. A shield-bearing warrior thrust his spear into the bony rib cage of a ram standing before the familiars, shattering it instantly. Now he had his eyes on Aldwyn and his companions. Apparently, their disguises were so effective that even Loranella's soldiers were mistaking them for the undead.

"Ahhhhhh!" yelled the warrior, charging with spear before him.

Aldwyn telekinetically lifted one of the severed ram heads littering the ground, blocking the weapon with a crack. But already a second warrior was swinging his pike at Lothar, who caught a lucky break when the spear's edge struck his chain. The soldier regained control of his weapon, but this time, before he jabbed at the wolverine again, Simeon jumped up and wrestled away the soldier's pole arm with his teeth.

"I hope you know I took no pleasure in defending you," Simeon growled at Lothar.

From behind them, one of the zombie tigers set his sights on the unarmed soldier. The beast made a running leap with claws outstretched, but Banshee vaulted herself off Orion's back and took down the bony predator in midair. She whacked the tiger with her drum. The soldier looked at her, stunned.

"Thanks," he said.

"This is getting complicated," said Gilbert.

The same human voice from before shouted out again: "Axe men, forward!"

Thirty of the queen's bravest flooded forth, holding their battle-axes overhead.

"Wipe away your disguises and get on Orion's back before Loranella's soldiers mistake us for zombies, too," said Skylar, as she shook her own body free of zombie entrails.

Aldwyn and the others wiped away the zombie goo as well as they could while the blue jay flew above them. Then they scrambled onto Orion's back. At Skylar's signal the lightmare galloped for the front line. His hooves sparked, leaving a flame-scorched path that incinerated zombies underfoot but also called a great deal of attention to their presence. Orion gathered as much momentum as he could before going airborne, soaring ten feet above the ground and straight over the soldiers. When the lightmare touched down on the other side, the animals found a hundred swords pointed right at them.

11

INTO THE ABYSS

A bearded man stepped forth signaling the others to lower their weapons. It was Urbaugh, one of Vastia's many wizards left magic-less by Paksahara's dispeller curse.

"These are the Prophesized Three," Urbaugh told his soldiers. Then he turned to the animals. "I see a wolverine, bloodhound, lightmare, and howler monkey among you. Go quickly. Collect the remaining descendants and bring them to the third glyphstone outside Bronzhaven. This one won't stand much longer." Then he turned to his men: "Tighten the line. Hold it as long as you can. The fate of Vastia depends on it."

Orion took them past the glyphstone, and Aldwyn spotted the ancient symbols carved into the stone pillar, covering the surface from top to bottom.

He couldn't help but think that if only they had collected the remaining three descendants already, they could have summoned the Shifting Fortress in Jabal Tur and tried to put an end to Paksahara's rule. That was followed by an even bleaker thought: if Skylar and Gilbert had been joined by Karna, the pocket dragon Jack should have chosen as his familiar, they wouldn't have been in this crisis to begin with.

As Orion galloped, he collected a remnant of the fallen city—a marble hand from a broken statue—and dropped it in his saddlebag.

"Can you believe that once—centuries ago—even before the time of Brannfalk, all of the land's greatest thinkers, artists, and warriors lived in Jabal Tur?" Orion said.

"None were more famous than a brilliant young warlock named Yajmada. He started a secret sect—what some called a cult—that would become known as the Noctonati."

Aldwyn noticed Skylar glance down at her anklet upon hearing the word. Lothar saw her, too, as Orion continued.

"Back then, just like now, there was a limit to how much magic it was believed one person or animal should have. This was a philosophy that some disagreed with, and none more outspokenly so than Yajmada. The king heard of his rebellion and gave Yajmada a swift and harsh warning. When the Noctonati kept meeting, the king had his soldiers burn their library. The warlock vowed that in return, he would ruin what the king loved most: Jabal Tur.

"Using all the forbidden knowledge that he had accumulated over the years, Yajmada constructed a suit of armor with four diamonds, each containing the essence of one of the four kinds of rain clouds. Together, these storm diamonds could summon a tempest that would destroy the city. The king foolishly thought the warlock's threats were empty. The ruins you see before you are proof they were not."

Aldwyn looked back at the ruins with new eyes. What he assumed was a city that had fallen into natural decline over time had actually been the victim of a battle over who controlled magical power.

"Thousands were killed, but Yajmada made one mistake: the king was not among them. Wizards from lands near and far were recruited, and together they tracked down the warlock. Upon his capture, the four storm diamonds were separated and kept under guard."

"I know how this story ends," said Simeon. "For hundreds of years, the jewels remained safe, until two dark mages, Uriel Wyvern and Jakab Skull, raised a Dead Army to overpower the strongholds that protected them. They succeeded in collecting three of the four storm diamonds, but before they could unearth the last, Kalstaff, Loranella, and the Mountain Alchemist defeated them. The diamonds were split apart once more, but this time they were not only guarded but hidden, their locations made a mystery. To this day they have remained unfound."

Aldwyn was quite certain that he had seen one of these very diamonds in the cellar at Stone Runlet, embedded in Yajmada's armor. Now hardly seemed an opportune time to share his discovery with the others.

The group was getting closer to the mountain now, and Aldwyn could see several large cave entrances. Piles of ore were stacked nearby, alongside abandoned mine carts.

Just then Lothar let out a howl. Everyone turned, but it was too late for the wolverine's cry to alert anyone to his whereabouts. Or was it? If there were zombies here, Lothar's heightened sense of smell would have detected them first.

"Who were you signaling?" Aldwyn demanded.

"I have no idea what you're talking about." Lothar raised his eyebrow to make it clear he was lying.

Then Aldwyn's ears picked up a noise from the direction of the mine entrances. He turned to see a dozen skeletal figures slinking out from the darkness and moving swiftly toward the familiars. As they got closer, Aldwyn could see that they were zombie cats. Not big ones like the great cats that had risen from the Chordata Plains. These were Aldwyn's size, some perhaps even from Maidenmere.

Orion stamped his hooves, preparing to charge. A confrontation appeared inevitable.

"Forget about them," Skylar called out to the lightmare. "Head for the Canyon!"

Unfortunately the only path to the crack in the Kailasa mountains was through this new attacking enemy.

Lothar, still shackled behind Orion, called out to the zombie cats, "Free me from these chains. I, too, am loyal to Paksahara."

Aldwyn could now get a better look at the cat who was leading the group. The spike poking through the rotting cartilage of the zombie cat's ear left little doubt about who it was.

Aldwyn was stunned. He thought he had seen the last of his traitorous uncle Malvern at the Crown of the Snow Leopard, when Paksahara's misguided blast had sent him to the Tomorrowlife. It had never crossed Aldwyn's mind that his uncle could come back from the dead to join the other animal zombies in Paksahara's army.

"Hello, nephew," said the zombie Malvern. "How do you like my new look? I think it really accentuates my cheekbones."

He turned to reveal that the flesh and fur once covering his face was gone, exposing nothing but bone.

Aldwyn could feel all his rage boiling up inside him. Malvern was the cat who had betrayed his father and murdered his mother.

"You know, I only had one regret the day you died," Aldwyn said. "I wish I'd killed you myself."

"Well, you've got your chance now," replied Malvern.

The zombie cat took a flying leap, digging a claw into Orion's hide and pulling himself up beside Aldwyn. He swung a bony leg at his nephew, his claw catching on the whisper shell necklace. Malvern pulled so hard it almost snapped free, but Aldwyn fought him back.

"You already took away my family once," said Aldwyn. "I won't let you do it again."

Malvern lunged out and bit Aldwyn's ankle, tearing at the flesh with his teeth. Aldwyn stifled a scream, unwilling to give his uncle even a moment's satisfaction.

Skylar flew over and started pecking at Malvern, while Gilbert began slapping at him with his

flower bud backpack. Aldwyn's cruel uncle was distracted by these nuisances for just a second, but it was enough time to allow Aldwyn to give a hard kick to the zombie cat's exposed jawbone. It knocked out a few loose teeth and sent Malvern tumbling to the ground.

Skylar took to the sky and began plucking bright yellow storm berries from her satchel and throwing them at the half dozen zombie cats standing in their way. Storm clouds immediately formed in the air. Tiny lightning bolts began shooting out from the clouds, one singeing Skylar's wing tip. The other lightning bolts struck the zombie cats, halting their attack. Orion kicked up his hooves and barreled past them, making a run for the Abyssmal Canyon. Aldwyn looked back at Malvern, who hissed at him from the dirt. There was little doubt that the two would be meeting again. Then the lightmare, with Lothar still in tow behind him, dashed into the crevice, leaving the zombie soldiers of the Dead Army behind.

The crack at the base of the Kailasa mountains was just three horses wide at the entrance but hundreds of feet tall. As they entered the Canyon beyond, it widened slightly, but not enough to get rid of the claustrophobic feeling Aldwyn was having of being stuck between two rock walls. Above, he could just make out a sliver of dusky sky. He felt like the entire mountain could come crumbling down on them at any moment.

Telekinetically removing a stretch of cloth from Skylar's satchel, he wrapped it around his bleeding ankle. Now the bite taken out of his ear would be joined by another battle wound.

"You okay?" asked Gilbert.

"Yeah," replied Aldwyn. "It's nothing."

"I wasn't talking about your ankle," said the tree frog. "I was talking about seeing your uncle."

"Oh, that. I'm fine." But even as the words came out, he knew that they didn't sound very convincing.

Skylar removed the Olfax tracking snout from the Mobius pouch. "Find us a white-tailed mongoose and a king cobra. Follow the same scent Grimslade had you track once before."

The nostrils immediately began sniffing the air.

"Gilbert, you hold on to it," said Skylar, passing

the snout to him. "If it starts tugging you, let us know."

"Am I the only one who gets creeped out by this?" asked Gilbert. The disembodied nose suddenly let out a loud sneeze. "Aw, and it's allergic to me, too. Just my luck."

"This is a brick that has fallen from the Bridge of Betrayal," said Orion, who had stopped to examine another artifact. "It has the markings of Brannfalk's throne." He scooped it up and dropped it in his saddlebag before continuing on.

"I get collecting shields and rare jewelry," said Gilbert. "But bricks?"

The lightmare smiled. "This is not just any brick, but one that dates back over two hundred years, and it tells a story as rich as any other artifact."

Aldwyn looked up at the steep walls and could see the peaks of the mountain high above them, blanketed in snow. He remembered how along with Skylar and Gilbert, he had crossed the Bridge of Betrayal. There he'd learned firsthand how quickly friends could turn into enemies when under the spell of the bridge's cursed stones.

They'd spent the night huddled within one of the mountain's caves, where they had discovered walls painted with stories of animal magic and had battled a cave troll that nearly crushed them.

Now, as they continued deeper into the silent Canyon, Banshee pulled out her drum and, first quietly, then more firmly, started to play. *Boom bah bah boom. Boom bah bah boom.* The sound resonated beautifully within the cathedral-like space.

Almost involuntarily, Aldwyn began to move his head to the beat, and he could see that the others did, too. It was a nice reprieve from the heaviness of everything they had endured on their journey so far.

"The howler monkeys in my village play the drums to communicate across vast distances," said Banshee. "But more importantly, they play to lift the spirits and feel at one with their heart-beats."

Her hands tapped the sides and top of her drum, coaxing a surprising variety of sounds out of the simple wooden instrument.

"Sometimes all it takes is a steady rhythm to

make life's problems go away for a little while."

The familiars were nodding along and getting swept up in the moment. Then the sound of Lothar's laughter wrecked the mood.

"What's so funny?" asked Aldwyn.

"I was just thinking about how much I'm going to enjoy telling the story of how the heroes of Vastia danced to the beat of a drum while the second glyphstone was being destroyed."

Through the narrow crack that led into the Canyon they could see a funnel of gray ash soaring up to the sky—the same thing that had happened when the glyphstone in Bridgetower had crumbled.

The sobering sight increased the urgency of their mission. Orion began moving faster again. Simeon continued to run at the lightmare's side, showing no signs of his age or fatigue.

Suddenly Gilbert's shoulder bumped into Aldwyn. The tree frog was trying to hold on to the Olfax tracking snout, but the force with which it was pulling him forward nearly threw him off Orion's back.

"Is this what you meant by 'tugging me'?" asked Gilbert.

Aldwyn reached out his paw and grabbed the gold chain, helping his friend tame the snout.

"Looks like it's trying to lead us down that gorge," said Skylar.

Aldwyn looked where she was pointing her wing and saw an offshoot of the main canyon that quickly twisted out of view. The animals turned and headed for the narrow passage. As they entered, the ground became sandier and the way darker.

Orion moved forward, following the snout, which was pulling them toward a fork in the canyon. The eastern passageway's walls were covered with crude drawings of white-tailed mongooses slaying king cobras with astral claws. On the western passageway's walls, the cobras were shown as the victors, overpowering the mongooses with blasts of venom shooting from their fangs.

Grimslade's magic tracking device was sniffing in both directions, tugging Gilbert back and forth.

"Now what?" asked the tree frog.

"The cobras must live in one canyon, and the mongooses in the other," said Skylar. "Let's split up and meet back here. Aldwyn, Banshee, and I will collect a mongoose. Orion, Simeon, and Gilbert, you'll retrieve a cobra."

"Whoa, hold on a sec," said Gilbert. "How did I end up on the team looking for the snake? Last time I checked, they were poisonous and enjoyed eating frogs."

"They do indeed have a reputation for being ruthless killers that shoot their venom blasts first and ask questions later . . . ," said Skylar.

"Not helping," said Gilbert.

". . . but they are also fair and noble, and I'm sure after they learn of our quest, one of their kind will join us."

"No matter how you cut it, they're still snakes," said the tree frog.

Orion had walked up to an ancient painting in the center of the divide. "Everybody, look at this," he called.

Aldwyn approached the picture and studied it more closely. Six animals—a bloodhound, a golden toad, a king cobra, a howler monkey, a wolverine, and a mongoose—were standing in a circle around a glyphstone, along with a man.

"This must record the time just after the lightmares left the First Phylum," said Orion.

"Look how their magical energy is all connected," said Simeon.

It was true: sunlight seemed to be shooting out from each of the seven in the circle, striking the glyphstone.

"So the Shifting Fortress could be summoned with a human," Banshee said with surprise.

"Look how well the different species work together," said Gilbert.

"Listen to you fools, reveling in its beauty," snarled Lothar. "All I see is the foolish, trusting eyes of those animals, who have no idea of the traitorous deception that man is planning. Can't you see that picture for what it is? An atrocity."

"I warned you once already about trying to breed discord among us," said Orion. "You will not poison our unity."

"I'd listen to him if I were you," Aldwyn told Lothar. "According to that painting, you can be replaced by a human."

"I wish that were the case," said Skylar. "But they're all channeling magic, and no human in Vastia possesses any right now because of Paksahara's curse."

Lothar flashed a smug grin.

"Come on," continued Skylar. "Let's hurry before it gets any darker in this canyon. Banshee, Aldwyn, come with me. We're going this way."

"What about the Olfax tracking snout?" asked Gilbert. "We can't both use it."

"I'm sure you won't need it to find the cobras," said Skylar. "They'll find you."

Skylar started toward the eastern passageway, with Banshee and Aldwyn following right behind her. Gilbert gave a nervous gulp and the others headed west, quickly disappearing from view.

As Skylar, Banshee, and Aldwyn traveled deeper into mongoose territory, they came across constant reminders of the feud these white-tailed mammals had with their reptilian neighbors. The snakeheads on spears were a first clue. Cobra skins nailed to the wall were further evidence of the bad blood between the two species.

"Not exactly the friendliest way to welcome visitors," said Banshee.

"Not if you're a snake, anyway," said Aldwyn.

"Well, luckily none of us have scales," said Skylar.

Peering into the nooks and crannies of the rocky walls, Aldwyn saw small triangular beacons of aqua blue light floating toward him. At first he dismissed them as freak reflections of the moon, but then the beacons sped up and headed straight for Aldwyn's neck and took hold. He stifled a scream and saw that Skylar and Banshee, too, had these strange, disembodied claws gripping their necks. They were in fact astral claws—sharp, blue, glowing blades attached to no hand or body.

"Spies of the cobras will suffer as they do," said a mongoose standing in the shadows.

"We don't stand with the cobras," said Aldwyn, choking out his words. Skylar quickly added: "We need one from your species for a mission of the utmost importance. We need a white-tailed mongoose to help ensure the survival of Vastia."

Another mongoose hidden in the darkness of the rocks, this one female, said: "Could she be telling the truth?"

"If you are in league with the fork tongues, we will put your heads on stakes, too," said the first mongoose.

The astral claws released their strangleholds, and several dozen mongooses emerged from the shadows. They were small and rather adorable; certainly not the kind of animal one would expect to battle king cobras.

One of the white-tails stepped forward. The long, gray hairs growing from his chin gave him the appearance of having a beard.

"You must forgive our caution," he said, and Aldwyn recognized his voice as the one they had first heard. "Our dispute with the cobras goes back centuries. They are a devious and untrustworthy band of belly crawlers. They eat their own young when they are hungry."

"And those are some of their nicer qualities," added the female mongoose.

"We need one from your clan to join us," repeated Skylar. "The evil hare Paksahara is trying to conquer all of Vastia. She will not spare any human or animal that defies her. Even here hidden away in the Abyssmal Canyon."

"We know about her plan," said the bearded mongoose. "Her minions tried to recruit us but we refused. I'm sure the same cannot be said of the cobras."

"I will go," said the female mongoose.

"But, Marati," the bearded mongoose started to protest. "We need you here. To help protect against our enemy."

"I'm sorry, Father. There is a greater enemy out there. I'm going to help these animals with whatever it is they need me for."

Marati walked to join Aldwyn, Skylar, and Banshee. Then she turned back to her clan. "But should I encounter any cobras on my journey, I will be sure to bring back their heads."

The mongooses all let out a cheer.

Aldwyn and Skylar exchanged a look. If Marati stayed true to her promise, their plans just got a lot more complicated.

12

POISON DARTS AND POCKET DRAGONS

Skylar and Aldwyn had taken the lead back down the canyon toward the agreed-upon meeting place at the divide. Banshee and Marati trailed a few yards behind them.

"You think it's time to tell Marati that she's going to have to team up with her sworn enemy to do this?" Skylar quietly asked Aldwyn.

"Absolutely not," replied Aldwyn. "Sometimes it's best to refrain from sharing all information."

"You mean lie?"

"No. More like not tell the *whole* truth."

Skylar shook her head.

"I guess you can take the cat out of Bridgetower, but you can never take Bridgetower out of the cat," she said. "And I mean that as a compliment."

The two shared a smile.

Suddenly, Aldwyn could hear laughter up ahead. It sounded very much like Gilbert. He came around the corner to see that it *was* Gilbert. He was sitting next to a large, dangerous-looking king cobra. Both were in hysterics.

"And I said, 'Camel? I know my jaw can open wide, but not that wide!'" hissed the cobra.

Gilbert was doubled over. "Stop, my stomach hurts. It hurts." He noticed Aldwyn and called him over.

"You have to come meet Navid," said Gilbert. "This guy's great. All the cobras are. We showed up and they welcomed us with open arms." He turned to Navid. "Well, not arms exactly."

At which point he and the king cobra cracked up again.

"Navid even knows where we can find a golden toad," added Gilbert. "The border jungles on the western edge of Vastia."

Just then Marati walked into view and Navid shot to attention. He bared his fangs, ready to strike. Marati lowered her belly to the ground and began circling the snake.

"What is a cobra doing here?" Marati demanded, never taking her eyes off Navid.

"I should ask the same question about this mongoose," hissed the snake.

"In order to defeat Paksahara, we need both of you," Skylar began to explain.

"If a mongoose has agreed to help on this mission, it is only so she can sabotage it from within," said Navid. "She cannot be trusted."

"He cloaks his lies with more lies," said Marati. "The cobras are the deceivers. And I will not stand for his false accusations."

Marati conjured her astral claws and took a swipe at Navid. The cobra dodged it and opened its mouth to send back a burst of jet-black venom. It landed a mere inch from the mongoose's feet, causing the sand itself to vanish upon contact.

Orion stepped between them.

"Enough," said the lightmare. "Your feud has

blinded you. This task is far bigger than your rivalry."

"Oh, but I am seeing perfectly clearly," said Navid. "I will go on this quest. Someone has to protect you from this traitorous mongoose."

"Your true nature will be revealed soon enough," replied Marati. "Then they will see you for who you really are."

"Good. It's settled," said Orion. "Now if you could just refrain from killing each other until the end of our journey, it would be much appreciated."

"Well, this will be very enjoyable to watch!" said Lothar.

Gilbert turned to Aldwyn. "I think I liked it better when it was just the three of us." Then he glanced over at Skylar and his eyes went wide. "What's that?" he whispered urgently.

"What's what?" asked Aldwyn.

Gilbert pointed at Skylar's wing, and Aldwyn saw the feather that had been singed black. It must have come from a lightning bolt during Skylar's storm berry attack on the zombie cats outside Jabal Tur.

"It's just like in my vision," Gilbert whispered to Aldwyn in full panic mode. "You remember my puddle viewing? The one where Skylar blasts a hole straight through me?"

"Gilbert, calm down," said Aldwyn. "It doesn't mean anything." But he, too, was wondering whether Gilbert's vision hadn't been so crazy after all.

❧

"If we wish to reach the border jungles by morning," said Navid, "I know a shortcut."

"A shortcut?" sneered Marati. "So you can

lead us all into a trap? No thanks."

"What do you think, Skylar?" asked Orion.

"We have to trust him," she replied. "Only one glyphstone remains standing. And time is not on our side."

Navid began heading toward a large hole in the far canyon wall. "Don't say I didn't warn you," said Marati.

She followed right behind to keep a watchful eye on the snake every slither of the way. Navid stopped before the tunnel entrance and looked closely at Orion.

"You may have to squeeze to get through some of the tighter spots," he said to the lightmare. "But I think you can make it."

Once inside the pitch-black tunnel, Skylar summoned a trio of illusionary torches to light their way. Navid led the group through endless sloping passageways. Marati braced herself for some kind of ambush around every corner. Once she even called out a warning that they were headed straight for the mouth of a tunneler dragon, but it was nothing more than a row of stalactites and stalagmites. The truth was that there were no hidden dangers lurking in this corridor. The only thing attacking the group was exhaustion.

"It might be wise for us to take another never-yawn nut," said Simeon. "We don't want weariness getting the better of us. Skylar?"

"I carried them in my satchel only briefly," she said. "Then I gave them to Gilbert."

"And I put them into Orion's saddlebag. I didn't want the nuts to get mixed up with my private snacks."

Orion poked his nose into his saddlebag.

"I don't see them," said the lightmare.

They all searched their bags, but none could find the neveryawn nuts. "Perhaps they slipped out while we were fighting in Jabal Tur," said Banshee.

"Seems odd. Nothing else is missing," said Skylar.

If the nuts had really gone, Aldwyn realized, the last leg of their journey had just become much more difficult. Without those nuts, they would have to continue on with no sleep, and they still needed to find a golden toad and get to the third glyphstone. If Skylar was right and the battle at Jabal Tur had nothing to do with the nuts' disappearance, then someone else had to be responsible. Someone within their group. Aldwyn looked at Lothar. But the wolverine had been chained up since his capture. That left only allies and friends as potential suspects. Perhaps all were not what they seemed.

<hr />

Navid brought them out of the tunnel on the far side of the Kailasa mountains. The trees and vegetation were lush. To the north lay the dry, arid landscape of Maidenmere, but here, nestled at the base of Kailasa, the sky was dotted with rain clouds, and a steady drizzle fell from above.

Aldwyn could only imagine how long this trek would have taken them had Navid not led them on a shortcut. Even Marati seemed to be quietly impressed by her rival's feat.

"So, Navid, where do we find one of these golden toads?" asked Gilbert.

"Keep your voice down," said Orion, pointing his snout toward twisting vines that snaked from tree to tree. "We don't need the chatter vines spreading word of our plans."

"The golden toads live among the palm trees," Navid said. "Feeding on the bugs that grow on their branches."

Banshee, Gilbert, and Aldwyn climbed onto Orion's back. Navid and Marati were offered a place there as well, but neither liked the idea of being so close to the other. So they chose to stick to the ground on opposite sides of Orion. Lothar continued to keep pace behind them.

Simeon sidled up to Navid and said, "I see the hate that you and the mongoose have for one another. What is the cause of such animosity?"

"The Abyssmal Canyon was the land of the cobras, long before the mongooses arrived." Navid's anger grew. "Before they slayed our king."

"Liar!" shouted Marati from the other side of Orion. "We were the rightful heirs to that land. We were only acting in self-defense."

"Whatever happened between your species in the past does not have to continue into the future," said Simeon to Navid. "Come. Let me show you something."

"What I just saw changes nothing," said Navid

a moment later. It looked as if the bloodhound and the king cobra had never left, but from the change in Navid's expression, Aldwyn could tell that they had just embarked on and returned from a walk into an alternative past. "You expect me to believe that those white-tails were merely innocents? You'd have better luck getting me to swallow an entire elephant."

Skylar sat by Orion's tail, looking out at the border jungles. The air was thick with moisture, and droplets of water clung to every leaf, branch, and twig. Lothar eyed the bird.

"Want to learn a magic spell?" the wolverine hissed.

She ignored him.

"It's a nifty one," said Lothar. "The kind your wizard would never teach you."

Aldwyn could see that Skylar was struggling to restrain her curiosity.

Lothar inched closer to the blue jay.

"It's called Yajmada's Spear," he said. "That's right, it was created by the founder of the Noctonati himself. I saw how interested you were in his story earlier. I figured you'd appreciate a spell that carries his name. It's a simple incantation, but one that needs to be spoken by a powerful spellcaster. You just say the words *astula Yajmada* and touch the tips of your paws, or in your case, wings, together."

Astula Yajmada. Those words sent a shiver up Aldwyn's spine.

"Do you think I'm a fool?" asked Skylar. "That I'm just going to perform some forbidden spell that might blast through your chains?"

"No, you're far too smart for that," said Lothar. "I just wanted to share with you a little taste of what kind of power you could unleash if you joined Paksahara."

Skylar looked at him scornfully.

"As bloodthirsty as you think I am," continued Lothar, "I bear no ill will toward my fellow animals. It is man I despise, and I think you do, too."

"I love my loyal."

"Yet they keep so much from you. Look what Paksahara has already been able to achieve since she left the queen. Commandeering the Shifting Fortress. Dispelling human magic. Raising the dead. Everybody has someone they wish they could bring back. Someone dear to them who is gone."

Aldwyn could see that this last note struck a chord in Skylar. He knew that the blue jay had long wanted to bring back her deceased sister from the Tomorrowlife, and now Lothar seemed to be offering her the chance to do it.

The group arrived before a patch of palm trees.

"Keep your eyes open for anything that sparkles in the light," Navid said. "A golden toad is not hard to spot."

Before Skylar turned her attention to the trees, Lothar got in the last words.

"Remember Yajmada's Spear," he said. "Try it sometime. That crimson blast never fails."

Crimson blast? Again Aldwyn remembered Gilbert's puddle viewing: it had been a ruby-colored spear fired from Skylar's wing tips that impaled the tree frog. One by one, the details of the vision were falling into place. Where at first it had seemed impossible, now it appeared almost inevitable. Aldwyn decided he would keep an eye on his blue jay companion from now on, just to be safe.

At that precise moment Aldwyn felt something sting the side of his neck. He looked down to see that he had been struck by a long, thin dart. Then he collapsed to the ground. He was awake and aware, but unable to move. One by one, the other animals went down, too, until all were lying motionless on the ground.

Aldwyn felt the blood pounding inside his forehead. Then he saw their attackers: a troop of very, very small hippopotamuses. They were gray creatures no taller than cucumbers wearing body armor and carrying blowguns.

"After everything we've been through—gundabeasts, seven-headed hydras, and thousands of zombies in the Dead Army—*this* is how we're going to die?" Aldwyn struggled to get the words out through his partially paralyzed mouth. "At the hands of a bunch of tiny little hippopotamuses?!"

"Tiny little hippopotamuses," repeated Gilbert. "Remember my vision in the pickle barrel? Those *weren't* sour dills! I knew it!"

"Look at that," said Skylar. "I guess all of your puddle visions really do come true sooner or later."

Suddenly Gilbert went pale.

"They do, don't they?" His eyes turned to Aldwyn and he whispered under his breath, "After Skylar kills me, I want you to have my poetry collection. That is, if the hippopotamuses don't kill me first."

Several hippos were closing in on them with giant netting, about to ensnare the animals, when suddenly a giant shadow swept along the grass. Its shape was unmistakable. It was a dragon. The hippo soldiers went into battle position, back to back and weapons at the ready. Then flames began to rain down on them, and they had no choice but to flee.

That's when Aldwyn glanced up to see that their savior was not a giant fire-breathing dragon but a *pocket*-sized one. Once the hippos realized what they had been spooked by, they stopped their retreat and turned their blowguns back at the little snake-like creature with wings. The pocket dragon reacted quickly. He might have been small, but he was fast.

As a volley of poisonous darts shot forth, the dragon let out fiery breaths, incinerating them in midair. The creature dipped down, sending

the hippos running as it strafed the ground with blasts of fire.

The pocket dragon chased off the last of the hippos, a few of them scampering into the brush with flaming rear ends. Once they were gone, the dragon landed beside the Three and the descendants. He reached into his pouch and sprinkled flower petal dust into each of the animals' mouths. It took only a moment for the paralyzing effects of the venom to fade away. Aldwyn's muscles loosened and he was able to sit back up.

"The chatter vines spread word of your arrival here," said the pocket dragon. He had a confident swagger that put the queen's noblest soldiers to shame. "I feared you would be easy bait for the Baroness's soldiers."

The brave little fighter reminded Aldwyn of Karna, the pocket dragon that Jack would have picked as his familiar if Aldwyn had not been there. After witnessing this daring rescue, Aldwyn was more certain than ever that Jack had made a terrible mistake.

"What is such a motley crew of animals doing in the border jungles?" asked the pocket dragon.

"We seek a golden toad," said Skylar. "The last descendant needed to complete the circle of heroes."

"Ha! The irony," said the dragon. "There is one in the possession of the very woman who just sought your capture. She is known as the Baroness. She's amassed a large fortune thanks to just such a toad."

"And do you know where we can find this woman?" asked Skylar.

"The Baroness lives atop Diamond Hill, so named for the precious stone found buried beneath it. But she will not part with her luck-bringing toad without a fight."

"Luck-bringing?" asked Gilbert.

"It is the golden toad's gift and their curse," said the dragon. "Just being in the mere presence of one can bestow good fortune beyond your wildest dreams. If a hundred arrows flew toward you, not a single one would hit. If you were dying of thirst, a geyser would sprout up from the ground at your feet. Old friends have been united, treasures have been found, and villains vanquished by sheer happenstance. That is why they are sought after by kings, wizards, and paupers alike. Unfortunately, the golden toad can't personally use its luck. That is why they are so easily captured."

"Can you point us in the direction of this Diamond Hill?" asked Skylar.

The pocket dragon lifted his wing to the west. "Just through there," he started to say.

"Looking for us?" a female voice called from beyond the trees.

A moment later a huge woman wearing finely embroidered clothes and an abundance of jewelry emerged. A golden toad rested on her shoulder, its ankle fastened to her by a chain. They were joined by a dozen armed hippos.

"It appears our luck just ran out," said the pocket dragon.

The Baroness stroked her finger along the toad's back, and a freak gust of wind was followed by the sound of wood splintering. Aldwyn and the other animals didn't even get a chance to move as thick tree limbs dropped all around them. Once the last of the branches had fallen, Aldwyn realized that he and his companions had been trapped within a dome-shaped cage.

"It seems my good fortune is your bad," said the Baroness.

The hippos raised their blowguns once more and took aim at the captured animals. Aldwyn felt another sting, this time in his thigh, and his body gave out on him. As his face hit the ground, he looked out beyond the cage and spotted Gilbert hiding in the trees. He was wide-eyed and trembling but free.

And now he was their only hope.

13

A STROKE OF LUCK

"There's good news and bad news," said Banshee. "Gilbert is out there, coming up with a plan to rescue us."

"So what's the good news?" asked Marati.

"That *was* the good news," said Banshee.

Aldwyn wanted to believe in Gilbert but couldn't deny that their situation looked grim. The captives had been brought to the Baroness's estate on the hill. Now they were being kept in separate cages within a large courtyard. And there were other animals here, too, held prisoners by the Baroness's hippo soldiers.

Even from the courtyard, the estate's spectacular

excess was apparent. It seemed that good fortune had poisoned the Baroness and her daughter with vanity. There were topiaries trimmed in their likenesses, marble statues, and portraits on silk tapestries that fluttered from every turret on the estate's grounds.

Unfortunately, a penchant for self-indulgence was not all that afflicted the golden toad's owner. The Baroness seemed to be paranoid as well. There were hippo soldiers in the watch-towers, and more patrolling the perimeter of the grounds with their blowguns. A Fjord Guard, a giant with blue-tinted skin and armpit hair that hung to his elbow, stalked the premises, making sure that no one broke in . . . or out.

Escape seemed impossible—and not just because of the tight security and the thick bars on the cages. Aldwyn and his companions also had to contend with the golden toad, who sat on a satin pillow before a high tower-balcony win-dow, sending bad luck their way.

That didn't mean Aldwyn had quit trying. He spotted the key to his cage dangling from a brass post standing across the courtyard. He focused his telekinetic powers on the metal key and lifted it into the air, pulling it toward him. Just before it reached the lock on Aldwyn's cage, a crow swooped in out of nowhere and snagged the key in its mouth. Then it flew off into the clouds. "It's no use," said Skylar. "Luck just isn't on our side."

"If I had a golden toad on my side, I'd bring luck back to my people," said Navid. "Put an end to our years of struggle. Allow every cobra to live in peace. Perhaps good fortune would rid our homeland of our enemies."

"Funny, I was going to say almost the same thing," said Marati.

"Look at that," said Navid. "For the first time a cobra and mongoose actually agree on something."

"I would take the toad to Split River and let it sit on my old loyal Galleon's shoulder," said Banshee. "That's someone who needs luck more than anyone else I know."

"The only thing we should be using that golden toad for is luck on this mission," said Aldwyn.

"We don't need luck," said Orion. "We have you, Skylar, and Gilbert. The Prophesized Three."

Not for the first time, Aldwyn's stomach sank at the phrase.

"Psst. Guys," a voice croaked. "Over here."

Aldwyn and the others turned to find Gilbert coming up over the edge of the estate's stone wall. He used his suction pads to scurry down it.

"Guards!" Lothar shouted. "Guar—"

But he couldn't get the rest of the word out. Marati's astral claw had gripped his throat and squeezed, allowing nothing more than a muted groan to wheeze out.

"Gilbert," said Aldwyn. "How have you not been caught yet?"

"I dunno," said the tree frog. "Maybe it's my stealth, ninja-like skills."

He hopped closer to the cages, tripping and knocking over a wooden noose stick.

"I have a feeling it might be something else," said Skylar.

"Remember how I told you that luck doesn't affect golden toads?" said the pocket dragon. "I would venture to guess it doesn't affect frogs, either."

"It would certainly explain why you were the

only one who wasn't trapped by those tree limbs," said Banshee.

"And how you made it all the way past the Baroness's guards without being seen," added Aldwyn.

"Gilbert, you have to go get the golden toad," said Skylar. "Until she's on our side, there's no way any of us are escaping."

"She's up there." Orion pointed his nose to the high balcony tower.

Gilbert glanced up to see the golden toad staring out the window.

"Okay. I can do this."

Gilbert readied himself and set off for the tower. Aldwyn, Skylar, and the others watched. The hippo guards had clearly become too reliant on bad luck to keep the Baroness's prisoners captive, because they paid no attention to the tree frog bounding across the courtyard. He made it to the bushes beneath the balcony and disappeared inside them.

Then after a moment, Gilbert popped up from the brush, making a speedy vertical ascent. He used the tangle of vines stretching toward the window as camouflage. Aldwyn smiled over at Skylar. Maybe their friend did have some stealth ninja skills, at least when it came to climbing.

Watching from his cage in the courtyard, Aldwyn could see Gilbert go up onto the balcony and begin talking to the golden toad. He couldn't make out what they were saying, but he saw Gilbert grab a decorative jewel-encrusted dagger off the wall and swing it at the toad's ankle. Without hesitation, the two were fleeing down from the tower window. By the time they hit the ground, a hippo guard had spotted them and cried out.

"The toad has escaped! Get her!"

All the hippopotamuses in the courtyard began running after Gilbert and the golden toad, aiming their blowguns. The first volley of darts whizzed past Gilbert and the golden toad, narrowly missing them. Before a second round was fired, the toad reached Aldwyn's cage.

"Stroke my back," she said.

Aldwyn stretched his paw through the metal bars and rubbed her shimmering skin. At that, their luck changed.

A sudden gale-force wind ripped through the still air. The strong breeze sent the newly fired poisonous darts flying back toward the hippos. Each one struck a different soldier, and one by one they dropped to the ground in a paralyzed state.

A single dart strayed upward, disappearing into a cloud above. After mere seconds, the crow fell from the sky with the dart in its neck. The bird landed at Aldwyn's feet with the key ring still in its mouth.

"Wow!" Aldwyn nodded to the golden toad. "You really are good."

He quickly used his telekinesis to unlock his own cage, then began unlocking the others'.

"Guys, this is Anura," said Gilbert, introducing the golden toad.

Aldwyn could already see stars in Gilbert's eyes. The tree frog had a crush!

"Follow me," she said.

The animals exited their cages. Not just the familiars and descendants but the pocket dragon and other captives of the Baroness, too. Banshee and Marati made sure that Lothar's neck shackles were put back on and attached to Orion's hindquarters.

Anura's gaze lingered on Aldwyn for a moment.

"You know, you look exactly like a cat that was imprisoned here. Except for that bite taken out of your ear."

"Us Maidenmeres all look very similar," said Aldwyn.

"No, the resemblance is uncanny. It's like she was your twin."

Suddenly, Aldwyn felt his heart beating in his chest.

"What was her name?" he asked.

"Yeardley."

If luck hadn't been Anura's natural talent, Aldwyn wouldn't have believed it. But the fact that crazy coincidences happened around her all the time left little doubt in his mind. She was talking about his sister.

"What happened to her? Where is she?"

"She was sold to a justiciary from the Equitas Isles," said Anura.

Aldwyn's head was spinning. His sister was alive and out there. He would find her as soon as he could. But first there was saving Vastia. And before that, getting out of the Baroness's estate alive.

The high courtyard walls were insurmountable for an animal as large as Orion. That meant the group had to leave the same way they were brought in: straight through the Baroness's house.

The inside was even grander than the outside. Crystal chandeliers hung above the long hallway, while countless paintings of the Baroness and her daughter covered the walls. Gold statues of them filled the halls. As the group followed behind Anura, Aldwyn was able to see into the dining room. There the Baroness sat at the head of a long table made of pearls and oyster shells. Her daughter sat at the opposite end.

"I want my lobster in bite-sized pieces!" shrieked the Baroness to one of the dozen servants tending to them. "How dare you make me chew more than thrice?"

Then the Baroness spotted Aldwyn running past the dining hall. She jumped to her feet and was about to scream when something got caught in her throat. All that came out was a gasp as she began to choke. She pointed frantically at the escaping animals.

"What is it, Mother?" her daughter asked.

"Do you want more lobster?"

Tears were streaming down the Baroness's face and she shook her head.

"Oh, dear," cried the girl. "She's choking! She told you to cut those bites into smaller pieces."

As her butlers and servants ran to her aid, the Baroness helplessly watched her precious good luck charm disappear down the hall, along with all of her prisoners.

Anura led them straight out the doors, into the estate's front yard, and toward the gates. The Fjord Guard caught sight of them and began to swing his sword.

Luckily his blade missed its targets and instead beheaded one of the Baroness's statues. The marble head went rolling as the animals continued their mad dash for the gate.

As the Fjord Guard chased after them, a sudden gust of wind tore a pennant from one of the turrets. The long strip of satin flew right into the giant's eyes. The blinded guard's heel landed on the rolling head and he fell like a freshly cut tree, crashing straight through the outer wall and slamming into the ground with a thud.

The animals sprinted over the fallen Fjord Guard's legs and directly to freedom. They didn't stop running—or in Skylar's case, flying—until they could no longer see the Baroness's estate behind them. Once clear of danger, they stopped to catch their breath.

After saying good-bye to their fellow prisoners, Skylar, Gilbert, and Aldwyn shared a moment of satisfaction. All seven descendants had been collected. If Paksahara and her Dead Army had not yet destroyed the third and final glyphstone, a chance at victory finally seemed within their grasp.

⁓⁓⁓

"I think I'm going to ask her out on a date," said Gilbert to Aldwyn.

"Aren't you moving a little fast?" asked Aldwyn. "I mean, you only met her an hour ago."

"Beauties like Anura don't come around every day."

"Well, don't let me stop you," said Aldwyn.

Gilbert puffed up his chest and started for the opposite end of Orion's back, where Anura sat talking with Skylar.

Night had fallen again. Despite their exhaustion, the group moved as fast as they could. Orion was carrying all but Simeon and Lothar, and the stalwart lightmare was beginning to slow down. The tireless pace of their march across Vastia over these last few days had taken a toll.

They had left the border jungles surrounding the Baroness's estate and were heading north to the Ebs River, which would provide the safest and swiftest route to Bronzhaven. That is, assuming they could secure or build a vessel large enough to carry all of them.

Gilbert hopped past Navid, Banshee, and Marati, then stopped behind the golden toad and the blue jay. He cleared his throat. The two turned to him.

"Excuse me," said Gilbert. "Anura, I wanted to ask you something."

Before the tree frog could finish, Skylar jumped in.

"Poor Anura," said Skylar. "She was just telling me how difficult it is being a golden toad. She barely knows someone for two minutes and they're already trying to use her for her good luck.

Everyone wants something from her."

Gilbert turned pale.

"You wanted to ask me something," said Anura.

"Yes, right," said Gilbert nervously. "Would you like some leftover maggots?"

He reached into his flower bud backpack and held out a webbed handful.

"Oh, thanks," said Anura.

She took the insects from him, and Gilbert quickly shuffled back over to Aldwyn.

"I think I will give it a little more time," said Gilbert. "I don't want to come on too strong."

Just then one of Orion's hoofs hit a large rock in the path, and the lightmare tripped, sending the animals on his back tumbling to the ground. As usual, Aldwyn landed on his feet. He immediately made sure that Lothar couldn't run off. Then he checked up on his companions. Fortunately no one seemed hurt.

Orion had gotten up again and turned to the others with an apologetic but drowsy look on his face.

"I'm sorry," he said. "I must have dozed off while

I was running. There's no way I should have hit that boulder."

"Let's stop for a short rest," said Skylar. "Even if it's just for an hour. If Orion takes another tumble, we may not be so lucky next time."

Gilbert looked to Anura.

"Or would we be?" asked the tree frog.

"We can't count on luck alone," said Anura. "Just look at the Baroness. She thought her good fortune would never end."

Despite the urgency of their mission, even Orion agreed that it would be best to take a short rest before their final stand at the glyphstone. Marati volunteered to keep watch over Lothar, while everyone else closed their eyes, including Aldwyn, who knew that he would need his energy and wits about him when the time came to face the evil gray hare.

14

TWICE BETRAYED

"He's gone."

Aldwyn opened his eyes with a start when he heard Banshee's panicked voice call out.

"Lothar. He's escaped," cried the howler monkey.

Aldwyn needed to look no further for proof than the empty dispeller chains fastened to Orion's back.

"How did this happen?" asked Skylar, who like the others had been jolted awake by Banshee's cry.

"I only closed my eyes for a moment," said Marati, looking sick with guilt and shame. "At least it felt like a moment. I'm so sorry."

"I knew it!" hissed Navid. "I told you she would betray us. The mongoose set the wolverine free."

"No," cried Marati. "That's a lie."

"Let's calm down for a second," said Simeon. "We don't know what happened here yet. This could have been an honest mistake."

"I checked those chains myself before I went to sleep," said Navid. "There's no way Lothar could have escaped them. Not without someone's help." The cobra spun toward Marati. "I say we chain her up before she tries to stab one of us in the back."

"How can I convince you that I'm innocent?" asked the mongoose. "Perhaps someone else among us had a motive for freeing him. Perhaps the same animal who threw away the neveryawn nuts. And if you remember, I was not even aware of their existence when they went missing. So it could not have been me."

"Whoever is responsible, arguing about it now is useless," said Simeon. "We need to plan how we're going to get Lothar back. Or track down another wolverine."

"If there's a traitor in our midst, we had better find out now," said Orion.

"But Simeon's right," said Skylar. "Our best hope is to find Lothar before he gets too far. We could use the Olfax tracking snout to lead us to him."

She reached a talon into her satchel and began searching for the nose. When she looked back up, Aldwyn could tell by her expression that there was more bad news.

"It's not here, either," said Skylar.

If Aldwyn hadn't seen Gilbert's puddle viewing and the blackened feather on Skylar's wing; if he hadn't overheard her conversation with Lothar about the Yajmada's Spear spell; and if he hadn't known about her past dabblings in forbidden magic, he never would have considered that his blue jay companion could be involved in this betrayal. But that's precisely what he was thinking right now. Accusing her here in front of everyone else seemed like it would have little purpose; he had no evidence, nothing more than a suspicion. If only he possessed the talent of telepathy, the ability to read minds, like his mother had. As it was, he would have to rely on his intuition—and he still wasn't sure what it was telling him.

"I don't know how we're supposed to find Lothar without that snout," said Gilbert.

"The mosaic," Marati exclaimed. "The one on the divide at the fork of our canyon."

"What about it?" asked Navid.

"The image of the circle of heroes," she said. "After the lightmare left, a human stood in his place."

"I don't know what her motive is," said Navid, "but Marati speaks the truth. The king cobras believed that there were eight descendants, but only seven were needed to cast spells together."

"That's fantastic!" said Gilbert. "We should be able to find a human in no time."

"Didn't you listen to what I said when we saw the mosaic?" asked Skylar. "We need a human who has magic. And all human magic is gone from the queendom."

The silence that descended on the companions was deafening. They had gotten so close, but now all seemed lost. Aldwyn had been right to fear the words Kalstaff had written: the prophecy had been wrong about him and his fellow familiars.

"Wait," said Simeon. "What if we found a traveler, a wizard who was not in Vastia or even the Beyond when the dispeller curse hit?" The others looked at him without hope. "Or a baby born with magical ability in the last week?"

They were farfetched, desperate ideas, but Aldwyn couldn't really blame the bloodhound for trying.

Then Banshee whispered: "Galleon."

Everybody turned to her.

Aldwyn was the first to understand. "Galleon lost his magic long before Paksahara's dispeller curse."

"Exactly!" The howler monkey was lighting up with excitement. "When he was defeated by Coriander in their disenchantment duel, his magic was channeled into a protective vial. If we can retrieve that vial and uncork it, Galleon could get his magic back."

"Now that just sounds crazy," said Gilbert.

"But it's also brilliant," said Skylar. "Paksahara's curse only affected those with magic when she first cast the spell. It would have no effect on

Galleon if he regained his magic now."

The way forward was clear. They would travel back to Split River, to the Inn of the Golden Chalice, and get Galleon. Then they'd see about getting his magic back. As to who the traitor was among them—*if* there was one—there was nothing that could be done about it now.

⸺⊷⊶⸺

The lightmare had the group on his back once more and was galloping with renewed vigor through the Hinterwoods.

The tall trees of the forest went by in a blur. Before Aldwyn knew it, Split River was coming into view for the second time on this journey.

"Ugh, I'm feeling sick . . ." Gilbert started to say, before catching Anura's eye. Then in an about-face, he continued: ". . . of how slow we're going. Come on, pick up the pace, Orion. You know how much this frog loves speed."

Swallowing back his nausea, Gilbert smiled queasily at Anura.

"Wow," she said. "Your stomach is a lot stronger than mine. I feel terrible."

"So do I," said Navid. "I've been nauseous since

we left the border jungles."

"Oh, thank goodness," said Anura to Navid. "I thought I was the only one."

Gilbert watched with a pained grimace as the golden toad and the king cobra bonded over their shared horseback sickness.

Aldwyn looked over to Banshee, who was nervously tapping her drum. The upcoming reunion with her loyal clearly had put her on edge.

"Everything okay?" Aldwyn asked.

"The last time I saw Galleon, things didn't end well," said Banshee. "What if he still holds a grudge? What if he doesn't want anything to do with me or this mission?"

"Then the world is lost," said Skylar, jumping in.

Orion reached the western edge of Split River and galloped over a bridge that connected the two halves of the port town. A lighthouse just offshore illuminated the nearby waters, which had a slew of derelict vessels stranded along its banks. Banshee knew the way to the Inn of the Golden Chalice, and she directed Orion there.

The streets were mostly deserted at this late hour, save for a few sludge diggers in filth-covered overalls who had fallen asleep on the sidewalk lining the city's row of drinking establishments. The animals arrived at the inn to find the tavern closed for the night and a sign reading NO VACANCIES on the front door.

"Banshee, do you know what room Galleon stays in?" asked Skylar. "I could fly up and peck at his window."

"His room doesn't have a window," said Banshee. "Not much of a view from the basement. There's another entrance in the back, though."

Banshee gestured to a skinny alleyway between the inn and a neighboring building, and Orion trotted toward it. As they got nearer, a voice could be heard singing.

"*Now I hold my nose / as the foul smell grows / that's the life of cleaning chamber pots.*"

As the companions turned the corner, they saw Galleon, dressed in a flannel nightshirt and apron, long underwear, and boots, standing next to a stack of porcelain bowls. He was dumping their contents into a hole in the ground while wincing from the stench.

"Hello, old friend," said Banshee.

Startled, Galleon dropped the pot he was holding, sending brown sludge splashing all over his boots. He looked up at Banshee, who was climbing down from Orion.

"Banshee," said Galleon. "And the rest of the . . . zoo. What are you doing here?"

"We're on a mission to save the queendom, and we need your help."

"*My* help?" he asked. "Do the Knights of the Realm need their bedsheets changed?"

"Paksahara's Dead Army has destroyed two of the three glyphstones," Banshee told him. "The only way to stop her is to gather the seven descendants around the last glyphstone. As far as we know, it remains standing, outside of Bronzhaven."

"That still doesn't answer why you've come to me," said Galleon.

"We need a wizard to complete the circle, and retrieving your magic seems to be the only way to do that."

Galleon shook his head and turned his back on the howler monkey.

"You said it yourself. I'm a fool. You'll be better off with anyone else."

238

"Cleaning pots and mopping floors. This isn't you, Galleon." Banshee walked around to meet her loyal's eyes once more. "The only thing that would be foolish is resigning yourself to this for the rest of your life. Come with us. Take back the magic you lost. Be the wizard I know you can be."

"I think you gave me that same speech three years ago. It didn't work then. . . . It's not working now."

But Banshee didn't give up. "I never stopped being your familiar, you know."

Galleon seemed to consider this for a moment. Then his shoulders slumped again.

"I'm sorry," he said. "I just can't be the hero you want me to be."

Just then, from the inn, the barkeep's voice called out: "Galleon, what's taking you so long? Go get your mop. Looks like Big Jim got food poisoning again."

Hearing this, Galleon untied his apron and tossed it to the ground. "All right. So what do I have to do?"

⁕

The animals traveled with Galleon to a cliff that hugged the Ebs. They crouched low to the ground

239

and looked out from the cliff edge at a majestic yacht floating in the river amid the broken masts of drowned ships.

"Coriander sails his yacht through Split River Harbor once a day," said Galleon. "Just to spite me, I'm sure. I know he's got some muscle on board. Elvin pirates. They come to the inn to drink and chuck tomatoes at me during my act. If you see one with a big scar under his eye, just know that he's got a really good throwing arm. Especially for somebody so little."

"We'll have to find a way to sail as close to the yacht as we can without being seen," Skylar said. "Then board it from the stern." She pointed to the back of the ship, where two of the pirates guarded a single rope ladder that led down to the water.

Banshee related the information to Galleon.

"Still the same know-it-all," said Galleon with a smile to Skylar. "You and Dalton always had that in common." Then he turned to the others. "I know where we can get a boat. There's a fisherman who frequents the tavern, and every night he sleeps off his cider on the inn floor. He never makes it back to his dinghy until morning. I'm sure he won't notice if it's gone."

"Let's go get your magic back," said Banshee.

They all rose to their feet. Aldwyn was careful to avoid stepping too close to the edge of the cliff.

"I'm afraid I can't let that happen," said Orion.

The others turned to see the lightmare staring at Galleon with a strange look in his eyes.

"Orion," said Gilbert. "What's going on?"

The lightmare lowered his head and began to gallop toward them. Everyone was too stunned to react. All Galleon could do was brace himself for the collision that would surely send him over the edge.

"The circle will never be complete," shouted Orion as he charged.

15

SLEIGHT OF HAND

Aldwyn strained his mind, lifting a nearby log and hurling it in the path of the oncoming stallion. It hit the lightmare, but instead of slowing him down, Orion crashed straight through it. Just before the horse barreled into the human, Marati conjured an astral claw and pushed Galleon out of the way. Orion dug in his hooves and came to a skidding halt, but the force of Marati's push sent Galleon flying. His body rolled off the cliff—but at the last second, his fingers grabbed onto the edge, preventing his fall.

Orion turned to charge again, determined to finish what he had started. Skylar flew up to him and began tugging at his saddlebag. Simeon, too, leaped up and clamped down hard on Orion's tail in an attempt to distract him, while Gilbert and Aldwyn tried in vain to hold back the light-mare's legs.

"Let go of me or I will kill you all," said Orion.

"Why are you doing this?" screamed Gilbert.

"We trusted you," squawked Skylar.

"Animals will rule once more," said Orion with a frightening coldness in his voice.

The animals had gained enough time to allow

Banshee to rush to Galleon's side and pull her loyal to safety.

Orion lowered his nose, and as Aldwyn watched, the lightmare's hooves began to spark with energy. He knew there would be no way to stop this mountain of strength.

Skylar tugged with all her might at the saddle-bag, ripping the strap just as the horse started galloping toward Galleon again. The bag hit the ground, the collected artifacts spilled out—and Orion froze in his tracks, a look of utter confusion on his face.

"What happened?" he asked. "Where am I?"

Everyone looked at the lightmare as if he was crazy.

"You just tried to kill Galleon," said a very cautious Gilbert.

"I feel as if I just woke from a dream," said Orion.

"More like a nightmare," said Aldwyn.

"Look at this," called Skylar from where the relics had fallen.

She was staring at the brown brick Orion had collected in the Abyssmal Canyon. On it was imprinted the image of Brannfalk's throne, the back and headrest carved in the shape of a blossoming tree.

"It's the brick from the Bridge of Betrayal," said Aldwyn.

Skylar turned to Orion. "Since you picked it up in the Abyssmal Canyon, you've slowly been infected by its curse."

Orion looked away. It appeared he was searching his own memory.

"My mind is cloudy. I only remember fragments . . . scattering the neveryawn nuts in the Abyssmal Canyon . . . and Lothar, I released him from his chains. I must not have been of sound mind."

The lightmare hung his head in sorrow.

"Gilbert, Aldwyn, and I have all felt the pull of the Bridge," said Skylar. "You can't blame yourself. There's no way you could have known."

She continued to stare at the brick.

"To think that a brick that had fallen into the gorge when we crossed the Bridge would come back to haunt us now," she said, deep in thought.

The others might have been relieved that Orion's apparent betrayal had been caused by an innocuous-looking brick, but Aldwyn felt a pang of guilt for having suspected Skylar of being the traitor in their midst. How could he have let his imagination get the better of him? She was an ally to the end.

"We're just fortunate that the leather strap of Orion's saddlebag tore when it did," said Marati.

"Thanks to our good luck charm," said Navid, looking over to Anura, who blushed in response. Aldwyn could see that Gilbert was none too pleased with their ongoing flirtation.

"Well, come on, everyone," said Banshee. "What's done is done here. We've got an old score to settle. Isn't that right, Galleon?"

The wizard nodded, appearing emboldened, as if the failed attempt on his life had given him back some of his old heroism.

The familiars and descendants walked up to Orion, but before they remounted him, the lightmare bent down on his two front knees.

"My deepest and sincerest apologies," he said. "From this point forth, I will never betray you again."

At this moment Aldwyn felt for the first time

that he was part of a true circle of heroes. Not because the animals were flawless or always brave, but because each was determined to do what was within their power to help good triumph over evil.

⁓❧⁓

"We'll be waiting here," said Orion, knowing they could not climb the rope ladder. He stood beside Simeon on the riverbank, wishing the others well.

The rest of the companions boarded the abandoned dinghy, which was beached partway up the muddy shore. Orion gave the boat a push into the river, and Galleon began to row toward Coriander's yacht, trying to avoid the overturned sailing vessels that filled the harbor. It was like crossing an aquatic graveyard, only instead of tombstones, torn sails and broken masts jutted out as reminders of what once had been.

They all remained silent, knowing full well how far sound carried over water. Most of the other sailors on this section of the river were not so intent on keeping their whereabouts unknown. A party was under way on a half-sunken skiff; Aldwyn could hear revelers clapping along to accordions and bag flutes, seemingly uncon-cerned by the crisis Vastia was facing. Farther along, another boat held equally rowdy passen-gers, who were standing at the rail firing arrows at seagulls flying overhead. As they drew close to Coriander's yacht, Aldwyn silently wondered if Split River would have been plagued by the same lawlessness and disorder if Galleon had retained his magic and stayed on as the town wizard.

Over the low metal railing surrounding the deck of Coriander's huge yacht, Aldwyn could see the tops of the elvin pirates' heads. The little buccaneers might have been fearsome foes, but their diminutive stature made them easy to sneak up on.

The ladder that Skylar had spotted earlier stretched down to the water. Galleon pointed out the two elvin pirates still guarding it, then nodded to Marati. The mongoose used her astral claws to push the pair of guards over the railing and into the water.

Next, Galleon lashed a rope around the ship's

ladder, tying it taut. He ran up the ladder and the animals followed. Banshee held Navid and Marati back.

"You two man the boat while we're gone," she whispered.

"Us?" asked Marati. "No way. I'm not staying here with him. I'd rather curl up in an ogre's old boot."

"That's appropriate, because you smell like one," said Navid.

"We don't have time for this right now!" Banshee swung up the ladder before the cobra and the mongoose could complain further.

Aldwyn looked back to see Marati walk to one side of the dinghy, while Navid slithered to the opposite side.

As soon as Aldwyn, Gilbert, Anura, and Banshee climbed over the railing and Skylar flew onto the deck, four elvin pirates armed with knives and miniature pitchforks came storming out of the galley with food still in their mouths.

"I think you all came aboard the wrong boat," said one of the pirates. "The Cyrus Brothers

Traveling Animal Show left harbor weeks ago."

The other pirates let out a gruff laugh. Their smiles quickly disappeared when Aldwyn telekinetically untied some rigging above them, sending a large wooden pulley crashing down on their heads.

The pirates flew into a rage, swinging haphazardly as they attacked. The fight took place so fast, it was hard for Aldwyn to keep track of it all. He looked to the left and saw Banshee disappear; to his right, Skylar was raising her wings. The next thing he knew, Banshee had materialized behind one of the pirates and was whacking him over the head with her drum, sending the little man facedown onto the deck. Then from over the side of the yacht came a murkman—a mud-and-algae-covered humanoid with webbed fingers and river sludge dripping from his gills. An elvin pirate lunged for the river monster with his pitchfork, but unfortunately for him, he had been fooled by Skylar's illusion and his momentum carried him right over the railing. A second later Aldwyn heard a splash as the pirate hit the water.

Only one pirate remained and Aldwyn noticed the big scar under his left eye. This was the ruffian Galleon had warned them about. The pirate reached into a bucket and lived up to his reputation, viciously chucking empty bottles at the former wizard. Although he had no magic powers to rely on, Galleon demonstrated an almost supernatural ability to avoid being hit.

"When you have an act as bad as mine, you get used to dodging things that are thrown at you," he remarked.

Aldwyn telekinetically stopped one of the bottles flying toward Galleon and sent it back. It hurtled through the air and smacked the pirate hard in the head, knocking him unconscious.

Just then the remaining three wooden pulleys gave way. They dropped with such great force that Aldwyn and his companions smashed straight through the deck. They fell two decks down, crashing on the floor of an opulent bedroom. Sitting on an equally opulent bed, a dashingly handsome young man and a beautiful young lady stared at the intruders.

"Talk about a fortuitous fall," said Galleon. "That's him."

The animals looked at Anura.

"What can I say?" asked the golden toad. "Things like this just happen around me."

Coriander jumped to his feet and pulled a jewel-encrusted scimitar out from beneath his pillow.

"Ah, Galleon. I expected to see you sooner."

"You have something that belongs to me," said Galleon.

"Are you referring to this?" asked Coriander, revealing a vial filled with what looked like a whirl-wind of smoke, hanging from a chain around his neck. "Or this?" he added, gesturing to the girl.

"I am here for my magic."

"Sounds like a rematch," said Coriander.

"Good. Perhaps it will be a fair fight this time around," said Galleon.

"Oh, I never said anything about it being fair," replied Coriander. "I suppose you've always wondered how I was so powerful when we first dueled. It was thanks to a little spice my father discovered off the coast of the Wildecape Sea. It's called fablehoot. And it makes you capable of things you never thought possible."

Coriander opened a small ivory box on the nightstand and took a pinch of the orange spice, bringing it to his mouth. Once he swallowed, his eyes began to shimmer with a silvery hue.

"Wow! That feels good."

Coriander cracked his knuckles and started circling Galleon.

Banshee took a step forward into the fray, but his loyal held him back.

"No," he said. "This fight is mine and mine alone."

Aldwyn and the others stood back and watched. They had barely blinked before Coriander was on top of Galleon, with the scimitar at his throat. He had moved with inhuman speed.

"Well, this isn't going to be any fun," said Coriander.

Coriander flipped the weapon upside down and, instead of slicing Galleon's throat, struck him on the side of his head with the brass handle.

He jumped back up and gave Galleon a moment to regain his wits and his footing. Galleon wasn't standing for more than a few seconds before Coriander was hitting him with a flurry of lightning-fast punches that sent the young wizard reeling once again. Galleon fell back on the bed. He wiped a trickle of blood from the corner of his mouth and turned to Delilah.

"Hello, my love," he said, as Coriander pulled him up by his shirt collar and flung him across the room. The airborne Galleon smashed into an ornate bookcase, sending it crashing to the floor.

"Think your chambermaid salary will be able to pay for that?" asked Coriander, mocking his foe.

Galleon brushed off the blow and attempted a running tackle on Coriander, but he was swatted away like an annoying fly.

"Every day as I sail this vessel through the Split River Harbor, I sit here and laugh at you." Coriander stalked up to Galleon. "Had enough yet?"

He kicked the former wizard in each side.

"Coriander, stop!" cried Delilah.

Coriander ignored her. He thrust his knee into Galleon's chin. Despite his opponent's spice-enhanced fighting skills, Galleon put Coriander in a headlock. But he had his arm around his enemy's neck for only a second before he was thrown back across the room.

"Now that was just pathetic," said Coriander.

Galleon lifted his head up from the floor and smiled.

"What in Vastia's name are you *smiling* about?" Coriander cracked his knuckles and sneered down at Galleon.

The young wizard opened the palm of his hand. In it lay the vial.

"It may just be a two-bit parlor trick, but sleight of hand does have its benefits," said Galleon.

Coriander touched a hand to his chest and realized that he had been stripped of his prized trophy. Galleon uncorked the vial, and the smoke immediately left the tiny glass container and snaked its way into his mouth and nostrils.

Everybody held their breath. Had it worked? Did Galleon have his magic back?

The wizard raised his palm and chanted, "*Danadium bendis!*"

The scimitar Coriander was still gripping bent and folded in on itself, turning into a useless lump of metal.

Galleon turned to the bed: "*Quipus animatum!*"

With a flick of his hand the sheets ripped out from beneath Delilah and twisted into a lasso, binding Coriander by his wrists and ankles. The villain struggled to break free.

"You're going to strike a bound man?" asked Coriander. "Not very sporting of you."

"Me? Oh no," said Galleon. "I always play fair. I'm going to leave you right here on your precious yacht. Just one more thing. *Nocturno infurious!*"

He conjured up a flame fairy, but unlike the small ones used to keep a campsite warm, this one was three feet tall and looking like a rabid beast. It shot down to the floor and burned a hole so deep that water started leaking in from two decks below. Aldwyn could hear a loud hiss when the flame fairy came into contact with the water.

"Hope you know how to swim," said Galleon. "Release!"

The bedsheets loosened enough for Coriander to be able to wriggle himself free. Water began rushing into the boat.

"My yacht!" screamed Coriander. "Do you have any idea the fortune this cost?"

"You can always get a job as a chambermaid," said Galleon. "I hear there's a position opening up."

Galleon took Delilah by the hand. Leaving Coriander to his fate, they all ran into the hallway. The boat was already starting to tip from the fast accumulating river water.

A grand staircase led to doors above. Elvin pirates gave chase, but Galleon blasted them aside with swirling wind blasts. They reached the main deck to find crewmen and elvin pirates in a state of complete panic. Some were fighting over the limited number of seats in the life boat while others were jumping overboard. As Galleon, Delilah, and the animals ran for the back of the yacht, the stern was sinking fast.

They started to descend the ladder, and Aldwyn could see Navid and Marati in the dinghy below fighting off the fleeing elvin pirates. Marati's astral claws and Navid's venom blasts were doing the job, but the force of the ship going under was creating whirlpools around the dinghy.

"Hurry up!" shouted Navid.

The animals and the two humans made their way into the boat. There was no need to even climb down the ladder, as the boat's top deck was level with the dinghy. Aldwyn could see Coriander standing there, his legs already submerged.

Galleon flicked his finger and intoned the words "*phasma vela.*" A big phantom sail appeared and caught the wind, allowing the dinghy to speed away.

"It's good to have you back," said Banshee.

"It's good to be back," said Galleon as he embraced his familiar.

Aldwyn watched as the two stood together, reunited at last. Although he had been apart from Jack for so much of the short time they had known each other, he had already come to appreciate how deep the lifelong bond between loyal and familiar could truly be.

16

A DESTINY MADE

The phantom sail carried the dinghy all the way to the shore and halfway up its muddy banks. Orion and Simeon were waiting exactly where they had been left. Galleon stepped out of the boat first in order to give a hand to Delilah. The familiars and descendants followed behind them.

"Go to the Inn of the Golden Chalice," Galleon told Delilah. "Take this key and wait for me there. I'll come get you when this is all over."

She nodded and looked into his eyes.

"We need to get moving," interrupted Banshee. "You two are going to have to save the swooning for later. For all we know, that third glyphstone is under attack as we speak. If it is destroyed, there will be no way to summon the Shifting Fortress."

Galleon reached out and entwined his fingers with Delilah's. The two shared a sweet smile, then the girl ran up the winding road that hugged the river and disappeared into the fog.

Once again, everybody climbed onto Orion's back; Aldwyn couldn't help but notice how crowded it had become. Simeon, who until now had been running alongside the horse, was encouraged by Galleon to join the others.

"I'm afraid you won't be able to keep up down there," he said.

With everyone safely perched on Orion's back, Galleon incanted, "*Longicaudum*." Then he shouted, "Onward, Orion!"

As the stallion began to gallop, his legs moved so rapidly they became a blur. His hooves were no longer sparking because they no longer even touched the ground.

"A swift step spell," said Gilbert. "I'm not going to lie. It's nice to have the skills of a human wizard back on our side."

And it most certainly was. A trip that would otherwise have taken half a day's time went by in a breeze. Orion ran along the riverbank, the water rushing by on one side, the trees on the other. Partway through their journey to Bronzhaven they crossed the Enaj but had no need to stop for a ferry or go searching for a bridge: Galleon only had to raise a hand, and the water solidified into stone, allowing them easy passage.

Aldwyn, Skylar, and Gilbert sat huddled together just behind Galleon. Gilbert leaned in close to his two friends. He looked at Skylar.

"There's something I have to confess," he said. "I had a puddle viewing in the stream outside the Gloom Hills."

"I'm glad you got that off your chest, Gilbert," said Skylar.

"I'm not finished," said the tree frog. "You were in the vision. You cast a spell. A crimson spear of energy came out of your wing tips." Gilbert paused for a moment. "It blasted a hole straight through me."

"What?" asked a shocked Skylar. "There must

have been some mistake. You don't actually think . . ."

"I did," said Gilbert. "And now I feel guilty for even having considered it."

"I would never hurt you. You're my best friend."

"I know. That's why I feel so terrible." Gilbert paused before continuing. "Sure, every one of my viewings has come true so far, but I choose to believe that this one won't. Maybe the puddles can be wrong."

There it was again: the way fate could be uncertain. Aldwyn was still wrestling with his own destiny and it seemed Gilbert was, too. The only difference was that Gilbert was convinced that his vision of being killed by Skylar would be proved wrong, while Aldwyn was not at all convinced that the prophecy that he'd save Vastia would be proved right.

"Gilbert, I will always stand at your side, and never willingly bring any harm to you," said Skylar. "Unless you continue to make me suffer through your poetry."

"Well, then, I guess you won't be hearing the

epic poem I wrote in your honor," said Gilbert.

"Okay," sighed Skylar. "Just this one exception."

"Really?" exclaimed Gilbert. "All seventy-six verses?"

⁓

Orion was racing across the lush green fields north of the Brannfalk Pass. A herd of emerald-hued sheep was stampeding past them, heading in the opposite direction.

"They seem terrified," said Marati.

"And why shouldn't they be?" asked Navid. "They're running from the Dead Army. Look!"

They came up over the next hill, and before them they could see that an epic battle was being waged in the fields outside Bronzhaven. On one side were the magic-less wizards and other humans fighting for the survival of Vastia; on the other, Paksahara's zombies, who were bent on destroying it.

Orion charged down the ridge and Aldwyn was the first to spot it. Pointing his paw to an area before the bronze gate where the combatants were most densely clustered, he said, "There it is. The third glyphstone."

He was flooded with relief that it hadn't fallen yet. There was only one problem: How would they possibly be able to get there alive?

"We should stop here," said Skylar, "before we draw any attention to ourselves." She lifted her wing and cast an illusion of a large tree for them to hide behind. Now they could survey the scene below without fear of being spotted.

Aldwyn tried to get a clearer picture of what lay between them and the glyphstone. They would have to pass through thousands of brain-plucked zombies: skeletal elephants and jackals, decomposing bears, the rotting great cats of Chordata, and waves of undead rams led by fleshless long-horned elks. Fighting with them were the living animal tribes Paksahara had recruited. Aldwyn spotted the warthogs he and his familiar companions had encountered in the Beyond, with their extra-long and sharp tusks. There was an entire slither of firescale snakes. High Plains mountain goats, wall-crawling dingoes, and, of course, wolverines. Chained gundabeasts were being led into the fray by cave shamans. There were opponents in the air as well. Spyballs filled the sky, covering the entire battlefield so no enemy of Paksahara could plot any surprises. Circling even higher, just below the clouds, were bone vultures, who came for only one purpose: to feed on the dead.

"Any ideas on how we might get to that glyphstone?" asked Gilbert.

"Let me at them," said Marati. "My astral claws will take down hundreds of those beasts."

"Not as many as my venom blasts," said Navid.

"I don't doubt either of your talents," said Simeon, "but the risk of losing one of you in battle is too great. There must be no casualties among us. We are the seven descendants. Every one of us must make it to the glyphstone."

"Unfortunately a stealth attack appears impossible, too," said Skylar. "I could cast another illusion, but the wolverines would smell right through it. And any other attempts would be seen by the spyballs."

"You could just try running," said Anura. "My luck might be enough to get us there."

"Sure, for them," said Gilbert. "But what about you? You said it yourself. Your own luck doesn't help you. Or me, for that matter."

"What if we used Aldwyn, Skylar, and Gilbert as decoys?" suggested Banshee. "I mean, technically we don't need them to summon the Fortress, right?"

"Us? Decoys?" asked Gilbert. "Terrible idea. Next."

"Even if we were able to cause a diversion," said Skylar, "how many would we be able to distract? One hundred? Two hundred? There are thousands down there."

"There's a spell Kalstaff taught me, called a force wall," said Galleon. "It's a variation of a force push, like a magic barrier. If I'm able to shape it into a tunnel, we might be able to run through it all the way to the glyphstone."

"Sounds like our best option," said Skylar.

The others nodded. Banshee turned to Galleon. "Let's do it," she said.

Galleon stretched his arms, facing his palms outward, and took on an expression of pure calm. The group watched as a translucent shell materialized on either side of Orion. Galleon's spell seemed to channel that energy forward, extending the force wall into a tunnel as he'd hoped.

Orion needed no prompting to start galloping forward. The lightmare stayed within the tunnel's protective shell, leaving the camouflage of Skylar's illusionary tree behind. They charged forward, through the first battalion of zombies. These were vicious close-range fighters, mostly bears and tigers. But their skeletal claws and teeth could not penetrate Galleon's tunnel.

Orion galloped through a second wave of Dead Army soldiers. These animals were more adept at jumping and attacking from longer distances. There were gorillas and what appeared to be jaguars and lions—it was hard to tell their species since their fur coating was now gone. The Dead Army didn't just concentrate their assault on the tunnel from the sides, either; they were coming from above, too. It was a good thing the spell was holding fast. The zombies were so brutal they were tearing each other apart in their mad attempts to break through the tunnel shell.

Their protection continued to extend ahead of them as it disappeared behind. But then a horrifying vision appeared in the sky. The clouds themselves began to reshape into the all-too familiar face of Paksahara. With a voice that sounded like thunder, the evil hare called out to her minions.

"Those animals on the steed must be stopped at once! Direct all your efforts at them."

The words were still rumbling in the air when every worm-eaten eye and empty socket turned to the galloping horse and its riders. The elephants aimed their tusks at the tunnel and stampeded toward it. Thousands of pounds of zombie might made contact, and the shell showed its first sign of vulnerability.

"This spell isn't going to hold much longer," said Galleon.

"I see I'm not the only one who's building an army of animals," said the gray cloud Paksahara. "Yours might still have their skin, but flesh and fur will be of no help in this battle."

"You hide in stained-glass windows and wisps of clouds," shouted Aldwyn. "But you'll be meeting us face-to-face soon enough. And when you do, it will be the end of you."

"Unlikely," said Paksahara. "Your circle of fools

will never bring forth the Shifting Fortress. And as long as it remains hidden, no one will be able to stop me."

Another coordinated attack of ivory tusks smashed against the tunnel, this time creating a tear. The path before them was no longer protected.

"It's breaking apart," cried Gilbert.

"Never fear," Paksahara called. "Once you're all dead, I'll bring you back as zombies and you can fight alongside me. If the bone vultures don't get you first."

Orion came to a stop. "The only way we get to that glyphstone now is by fighting," he said.

Marati readied her claws and Navid bared his fangs, standing upright in strike position. Orion's hooves began sparking. Aldwyn steadied his mind, preparing to use his telekinesis in any way he could.

The first zombie animal to break through the tear in the protective shell was one of the rams. It was coming at them when suddenly an axe flew through the air and landed with a bone-crunching thud right between the ram's ears. Aldwyn spun around to see a dozen of Queen Loranella's royal guardsmen riding up on the lightmares from the Yennep Mountains. The bearded warrior Urbaugh was riding Galatea.

"Follow me," Urbaugh yelled.

Orion started to gallop after Galatea. But Urbaugh was taking them away from the glyphstone.

"You're going the wrong way," shouted Skylar.

"Don't worry," said Galatea. "We'll get you where you need to go."

Aldwyn wasn't exactly sure what the leader of the lightmares had in mind: she and the other horses were most definitely galloping farther and farther away from the magic stone.

"Let them run away," Paksahara shouted, commanding her army from the sky. "Finish what you started. Destroy that pillar!"

The zombies immediately raced toward the glyphstone, making escape easier. Aldwyn's bewilderment kept growing. Urbaugh and Galatea led them across the field and beyond a grove of trees to an encampment. Tents had been erected around an old broken-down windmill, and it was here that Aldwyn saw that it was not just humans who had united on the side of the queen: animals who had refused to join Paksahara's cause were present as well. Urbaugh and Galatea brought them to a stop before the largest of the tents.

"I have the Prophesized Three," Urbaugh called out. "And they have collected all seven of the descendants."

The flap of the tent was folded back, and none other than Queen Loranella herself stepped out.

"How wonderful," she said with tears of pride in her eyes. "I knew you would succeed in your quest."

"We have succeeded in nothing yet," said Skylar. "And if the glyphstone behind us falls, you may as well hand Paksahara the throne."

Aldwyn was amazed at how calm the queen was. He looked back and could see through the grove of trees that Paksahara's army had gotten through the final line of soldiers protecting the glyphstone. And the mighty gundabeasts led by the cave shamans were making their way forward to destroy it.

"There must be some way to go back," said

Aldwyn. "We can't just let the third glyphstone fall."

But alas, it was too late. All turned upon hearing the thundering roar of the gundabeasts. They watched as the three-eyed creatures barreled ahead to topple the stone pillar. Then Aldwyn saw something miraculous happen. As the fists of the beasts struck, the glyphstone evaporated, dissipating as if it was one of Skylar's illusions. No funnel of gray ash rose into the sky.

"I don't understand," said Gilbert.

Just then a flock of birds—hundreds of them—including two very recognizable blue jays, flew into the center of the camp.

"Mom! Dad!" exclaimed Skylar.

It was the birds from the Nearhurst Aviary. Not only were Skylar's mom and dad there, but also the nightingale Hepsibah and Skylar's childhood friend, the cardinal Mason. These were all birds trained in the art of illusion, and the fake glyphstone must have been their cleverest trick yet.

"Wait," said Skylar. "If the glyphstone wasn't there, then where is it?"

With a wave of her wing, Hepsibah made the decrepit windmill disappear. The familiars gasped when they saw what actually lay beneath it: the last glyphstone, standing tall, proud, and right before them.

"You need to hurry," said Queen Loranella. "Paksahara won't stay fooled for long. She'll be sending her army here right now."

The descendants wasted no time. One by one, they took their places in a circle around the pillar. Aldwyn, Skylar, and Gilbert stood with the queen and watched as they assembled: Banshee the howler monkey, Simeon the bloodhound, Orion the lightmare, Marati the white-tailed mongoose, Navid the king cobra, Anura the golden toad, and Galleon the human wizard.

The circle of heroes stood side by side, hand in paw and tail wrapped around leg. As they became connected, a bright sunlight-colored aura started glowing around them; then orange rays burst forth from the seven, striking the glyphstone. The runic symbols covering the pillar began to sparkle as if a magic deep within the boulder was being awakened.

Aldwyn felt as if he could finally put to rest his fear about fulfilling the prophecy.

"Back at Stone Runlet," he said to the others, "I read something in Kalstaff's diary. He said that prophecies don't always come true. I was afraid that the stars had made a mistake. That Jack had chosen the wrong familiar. That we'd fail. But I guess the stars had a plan after all."

"It wasn't the stars that made the prophecy come true," said Queen Loranella. "It was the three of you. Everybody makes their own destiny."

Across the field, a giant smoky-blue globe appeared. Hundreds of feet up in the air, the top floor of a tower materialized, followed by a curving staircase that led up to it. Then, like an intricate patchwork, one brick after another appeared, creating the tower's smooth, gray outer walls and base. Veins of red stretched from its bottom to its peak, throbbing as if they were alive.

"The Shifting Fortress," said Aldwyn.

They had brought it back.

17

BATTLE AT BRONZHAVEN

The descendants remained in a circle. The glyphstone was still glowing, but there was no longer any light streaming from the descendants.

"You can step back now," said Queen Loranella. "The summoning spell is complete."

The queen signaled a chinchilla that was sitting nearby, and the brown ground rat, with its big ears and protruding whiskers, crawled up her arm and onto her shoulder. It opened its tiny mouth and proceeded to let out a deafening roar.

The trumpeting sound seemed to be a gathering call. Once its echo spread through the maze of neighboring tents, more allies of the queen emerged into the open. There were hundreds of cloaked warriors, wearing different-colored robes, each bearing the crest of one of Vastia's ten provinces. Carrying swords and staves, they gathered before the queen in orderly lines, awaiting her command.

"I see you devised a shrewd battle plan," said Galleon.

"Yes, I only sent a fraction of our forces to protect the illusionary glyphstone," said Queen Loranella. "I knew that once the Fortress was summoned, we would need the majority of our troops here."

Out of a separate tent came a man with curly red hair who Aldwyn knew as the shopkeeper from the familiar store in Bridgetower. He was joined by a menagerie of magical animals, many of which Aldwyn recognized from his brief stay in the shop. There were teleporting wombats, tiny lizards with saddles on their backs, large-eyed lemurs, poisonous hedgehogs, and more.

"Dad, Phillip, what are you doing here?" asked a surprised Gilbert.

Aldwyn turned to see a mass of Daku tree frogs approaching, including Gilbert's dad and his brother Phillip. They were all armed with spears, but unlike the ones they had used in previous battles, these were thicker and made of bamboo, each with unique symbols carved into them.

"We've come to fight alongside you, brother," said Phillip.

"And we brought you this," said Gilbert's dad.

The elder tree frog held out a spear for Gilbert, who took it with great pride.

"My valor staff," he said, and Aldwyn thought he could glimpse a tear in his companion's eyes. Gilbert promptly strapped it to his back.

Then Sorceress Edna pushed through the crowd, holding a porcelain piccolo in her hands. Urbaugh and the other royal guardsmen stood beside Loranella.

"Soldiers of Vastia, defenders of this land," said the queen. "There are two tasks that remain before us. One is to defend this pillar. As long as it stands, the Shifting Fortress will be unable to move from this location. The other is to infiltrate the tower itself. You won't see a door and the only window is at the very top—in the casting chamber. The only way to get inside is to conjure a telegate. The casting chamber is where you will find a receiving vessel that holds all of the dispelled magic taken from Vastia's wizards. You must destroy it to reverse the disenchantment."

"I've seen what she's talking about," Aldwyn said quietly to Skylar. "Through the eye of one of the spyballs. A giant crystal urn filled with wisps of smoke, much like the vial that Coriander wore around his neck."

Meanwhile, Queen Loranella had continued issuing her commands. "Urbaugh, take the rangers of the Estovian province and the mace-wielders from the Crescent Islands. Try to carve a path to the tower."

Urbaugh nodded and began gathering a faction of black-hooded men and women with shaved heads. The queen turned to the guardsman sitting atop Thisby, one of the lightmares who had competed on the Scorch Path. The guardsman had dark black eyebrows and a thick mane of hair pulled back in a ponytail.

"Commander Warden," continued Loranella. "Take your pupils from Turnbuckle Academy and make a run for the Fortress. Familiars, descendants, do the same. My friends from Nearhurst, spread yourselves among the troops. Your illusions are an asset to all. Tree frogs, you'll stay here and guard the glyphstone along with the Bronzhaven shield-bearers."

Paksahara's zombie army was mobilizing its own plan of attack, with one half of it poised to defend the Shifting Fortress, and the other marching toward the glyphstone. Spyballs were looming overhead, watching every move of the queen's army. That's when Sorceress Edna used her piccolo to send out a melodic call. Within seconds Aldwyn felt the air starting to vibrate. A flock of tremor hawks thundered across the sky. The spyballs were unprepared for the swift attack, and it became readily apparent that these winged eyeballs were a tasty treat for the hawks, who began to gobble them up.

Aldwyn and his companions were hurrying

through the encampment to where the trees began. "I think we should split off from here," said Orion. "I'll draw the Dead Army's attention away from you."

He nodded to Mason, who was perched in one of the trees.

"Come, red bird," he said. "Let's put your illusionary skills to work."

Mason flew toward them and landed on the lightmare's back, then gave a wink to Skylar before Orion galloped off into the trees. The familiars and Navid, Banshee, Marati, Galleon, and Simeon took a different path, stalking through the apple trees, while all around them, beyond the forest, the noise of battle could be heard. They continued on, over knobby roots and around shallow pools of quickmud. Aldwyn's eyes never lost sight of the tip of the Fortress peeking out above the trees.

"Has anyone seen Anura?" asked Gilbert.

The others glanced around. Just as the realization was sinking in that they'd somehow managed to lose Anura in all the chaos, they heard a mighty crash up ahead. A twenty-foot-tall gundabeast broke through the trees before them, its three eyes bloodshot and angry, its horn sharp enough to pierce any armor. Chains were wrapped around its waist, and behind it a cave shaman with a sparking electrical whip prodded the creature.

"Attack!" the tongueless shaman hissed through the hole in his throat.

Galleon conjured a bolt of fire, and Marati and Navid delivered attacks of their own, but all merely bounced off the thick plating encasing the vicious beast's hide.

"Whew, I thought I'd lost you," said Anura, bouncing up to the others. "I just got stuck in some quickmud."

And just like that, their luck changed. Suddenly constrictor vines reached out and grabbed the gundabeast by its wrists and ankles. Another tangle of vines took hold of the cave shaman and lifted him off his feet, making him disappear from view.

"That's what I would call good fortune," said Aldwyn. "It seems those constrictor vines sprang out at just the right moment."

Gilbert turned to Anura.

"More like *you* turned up at just the right moment," he said to the golden toad. "I'm not sure I ever want to leave your side."

Anura blushed.

Gilbert blushed.

"No, no. I didn't mean it like that," blurted out the tree frog. "I mean, unless you wanted me to. Okay, I'm going to stop talking now."

With the gundabeast held captive by the vines, the familiars and descendants made their way out of the woods and onto the battlefield, where Urbaugh and his troops were slashing their way through a pack of undead long-horned elk. Urbaugh was slicing two heads off at a time with his sword while the rangers beside him fired arrows at the zombie attackers. In front of them, Commander Warden and the young wizards of Turnbuckle Academy, who looked no older than Marianne or Dalton, were clearing a path toward the Fortress. They each had a familiar at their side casting spells and using their innate magical talents to fight back the dead hordes. Warden himself looked to be a superb leader, directing his pupils in wave after wave of coordinated attacks.

Aldwyn turned to see Orion galloping through enemy forces. On the lightmare's back was a perfect illusion being cast by Mason. Aldwyn and the others appeared to be riding atop the horse. They were drawing a tremendous amount of attention from Paksahara's minions, both living and dead, and the few spyballs that were left after the tremor hawk assault. Mason was causing a distraction, drawing attention away from Aldwyn and the others.

The familiars and descendants used the diversion as an opportunity to move forward. Keeping low to the ground, Aldwyn was beginning to think that they might be able to make it to the Shifting Fortress without having to engage in this lethal battle. Then he heard the pained howl of Simeon behind him. He spun around to see Lothar attacking the bloodhound, who struggled beneath the weight of the wolverine and three of his companions.

"That illusion may have fooled the zombies, but your scent is unmistakable," snarled Lothar. "Nothing compares to the real thing."

Aldwyn focused on a nearby boulder and telekinetically sent it flying through the air, knocking the wolverines clear off Simeon. They quickly got back on their feet and began circling. The old bloodhound lay there, badly wounded and hardly breathing.

Galleon stepped forward.

"Go," he said to the animals. "I'll handle this."

Aldwyn and the others hesitated.

"A *human* risking his life for an animal?" asked Lothar, his voice dripping with hate. "Be not fooled, my four-legged brothers. It is nothing but cowardice—staying back to fight us rather than forging ahead against even greater odds."

"You're wrong," said Banshee. "You've never had a loyal, so you don't know the meaning of the word."

The howler monkey walked up to Galleon's side.

"Continue on, Banshee," said the wizard. "I'll be okay."

"No. We stand together."

"Human and animal will never stand together," said Lothar. "Man will always betray us in the end."

The wolverine leaped forward, baring his claws.

Banshee turned invisible while Galleon chanted: *"Trussilium bindus!"*

A silver rope materialized in his hand, and he threw the coiled end around Lothar's ankle. While Banshee and Galleon grappled with the wolverines, Aldwyn, Skylar, Gilbert, Anura, Navid, and Marati ran on.

The clouds above rumbled again and the image of Paksahara was smiling deviously down at them.

"You're losing, Loranella," the hare's voice called out. "What have you accomplished? Ridding me of my spyballs? I'll just summon more of them. Fighting off some of my Dead Army? There are thousands more corpses to raise. The glyphstone will fall, and once it does, you'll never find me again."

Aldwyn turned back and could see in the distance that the first of the zombie elephants had reached Loranella's encampment. He made out what looked like small green dots jumping on top of them, and though the view wasn't clear, he knew that the Daku tree frogs were using their ninja-like abilities to defend the still-glowing glyphstone. And it seemed they were being assisted by the shopkeeper's assortment of familiars, too.

But Paksahara's taunts were not entirely unwarranted. Though her undead hordes had not yet toppled the pillar, they were beginning to push back Urbaugh's and Warden's assault on the Fortress. The Turnbuckle wizards were being overwhelmed. Not only were they combating the zombies, but now living animals loyal to Paksahara—like the firescale snakes and warthogs—had entered the fray. Warden was doing all he could to help, but without magic, he was just a man.

"We can't leave the young wizards behind," said Gilbert.

"If someone doesn't make it into the Shifting Fortress soon, many more innocent lives will be lost," said Skylar.

Aldwyn was torn. He agreed with Gilbert but also knew that Skylar was right.

"Besides, if their own familiars can't help them, neither can we," said Navid.

"That may not be entirely true," said Anura. "Go ahead without me. I'll stay back with them."

She turned to Gilbert. "Maybe you can recite some of your poetry for me, you know, when this is all over."

Gilbert smiled. "I'd like that."

The golden toad hopped across the battlefield, and as she approached the young wizards, one of the firescales sent out a blast headed straight for Loranella's army. But as luck would have it, the flames went off course, hitting a patch of dry grass. In an instant the ground caught fire, melting the zombies and causing the living animals to retreat.

⁓

The familiars and the last two of the descendants—Navid and Marati—didn't have far to go before reaching the Fortress. But Paksahara's defenses were becoming ever more impenetrable. Several skeletal wolves came charging at them. Navid and Marati were fast to react: Navid taking out two with his venom blasts, Marati another with her astral claws. Gilbert pulled the valor staff from his back and lunged at one of the wolves, but the bamboo spear only grazed its bony target. Then, before Skylar or Aldwyn could do anything, Gilbert was swallowed by the zombie wolf.

"No!" shouted Aldwyn. He was almost too stunned to react.

The skeletal wolf that had swallowed Gilbert had no flesh or fur, only bones, and the tree frog could be seen trapped within the creature's rib cage. He was shaking the bones as if they were the bars of a prison cell.

"Somebody get me out of here," screamed Gilbert. "Help!" Skylar reached into her satchel and grabbed a bright yellow storm berry. She flew over the undead wolf and had to dodge its claw as she dropped the berry, causing a dark cloud

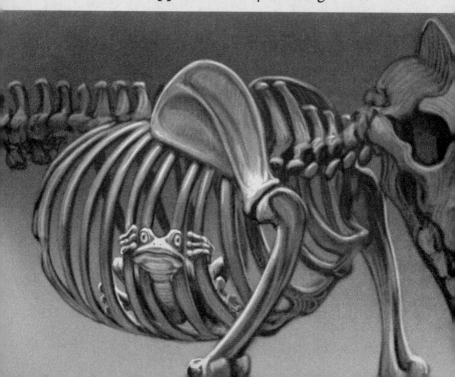

to appear. A lightning bolt shot out, striking the skeleton's torso and shattering its bones. Gilbert was freed, falling to the ground.

"Who knew these storm berries would come in so handy?" Skylar asked.

Aldwyn, Skylar, Navid, and Marati were starting to move forward again, but Gilbert was still picking himself up and strapping his staff back over his shoulder. He looked down at a puddle that had formed from the berry's impromptu storm. The tree frog leaped to his feet and pushed Aldwyn away from the muddy patch on which he was standing. Just as he did, a magical flaming arrow shot down from the tower, striking the spot where Aldwyn had been only a moment before.

"Gilbert, how did you know?" asked Aldwyn.

"I saw it in the puddle," replied Gilbert.

Another volley of fiery arrows came raining down, narrowly missing the animals but setting the earth around them on fire.

"You need to guide us the rest of the way," said Skylar.

"How am I supposed to do that?" asked Gilbert.

Skylar dipped her beak back into her satchel

and removed another bunch of storm berries. She threw them in a line leading to the Fortress, creating a path of storm clouds that left puddles of rain all the way to the tower. Gilbert glanced down into the first, and Aldwyn too caught a glimpse of the vision that appeared: more flaming arrows striking the ground in a zigzag pattern. Aldwyn looked up to see that same ground before them, yet to be bombarded with fire from above.

Gilbert leaped forward, bounding from side to side, anticipating where the next attack would land. The others followed, and as long as they stepped where Gilbert did, they avoided the rain of fire from above. The same couldn't be said for the zombies chasing them, who became unwitting targets of the blast. Clearly Paksahara hadn't been kidding when she said her Dead Army soldiers were disposable.

Amazingly, the familiars reached the outside wall of the Shifting Fortress unharmed. Aldwyn was awed by the tower's height. From a distance it had looked large, but up close he got his first true sense of just how tall the structure really was. As Loranella had said, there was no door, and they couldn't reach the window in the casting chamber. Aldwyn could see that the walls were perfectly smooth, save for one cornerstone that was mysteriously absent. At the top of the tower Aldwyn could see what looked like a sculpted stone lion's head, its mouth agape. Obsidian powder poured out from it, calling Skylar's attention to it as well.

Despite the mess of shattered bones behind them, more zombies were on their way.

"Now might be a good time to conjure that telegate," said Aldwyn.

"I'm working on it," said Skylar.

She reached into her satchel again and removed several different components and objects.

"Seashell, dust mites, herbs, lead weight, open up a telegate!" The blue jay's chant was urgent.

She let the spell's ingredients fall to the ground, and at once a gateway materialized on the surface of the wall. As Paksahara's undead minions continued to march toward them, the five animals jumped through the opening, into the Shifting Fortress.

18

THE SHIFTING
FORTRESS

O nce inside, Skylar, Aldwyn, Gilbert, Navid, and Marati found themselves in a giant square room with a spiral staircase leading upward. Below them, an enormous blue globe was spinning and rotating in the glass floor. As it turned, Aldwyn could have sworn he was able to catch glimpses of other parts of the world, presumably all the different places the Fortress could shift to.

The telegate was closing, but before it shut completely, a dozen ferocious jackal zombies managed to slip through. Then the portal disappeared.

One of the jackals propelled itself toward Marati, but Navid shot out a venom blast that made the zombie's bones disappear in midair.

"Go ahead," Navid called to the familiars. "Marati and I will take them."

"After all we've been through, now you decide to reveal yourself for who you truly are?" said Marati.

"What's that?" asked Navid.

"A friend," Marati said. "Now let's see which one of us can send more of these ugly beasts back to their graves."

Standing back to back, the king cobra and white-tailed mongoose used venom and claw to fight off their attackers, while the Three ran for the stairs.

The sound of Navid and Marati doing battle faded fast as the three familiars reached the second floor of the Shifting Fortress. The huge room had ceiling-high shelves crammed with spell scrolls, more than Aldwyn had ever seen in any one place. Although there were no windows, the library was brightly lit by the multicolored flames of Protho's Lights. Painted portraits of the previous kings and queens of Vastia hung on the walls, and it appeared to Aldwyn as if they had recently been slashed.

Aldwyn, Skylar, and Gilbert moved swiftly across the chamber to the next flight of stairs, racing to the tower's third story. Here they found a room cluttered with alchemical tools: vials and beakers swirling with differently colored liquids; worn cabinets that smelled of the thousands of herbs and flowers stored inside; and a large cauldron bubbling with who-knew-what inside. Glass tanks held hideous evidence of Paksahara's early failed attempts at raising the dead.

The familiars never slowed down, continuing on to the fourth floor, which seemed to be the evil hare's command center. A map covered an enormous table, with ruby-headed pins charting the Dead Army's progress across the land. One stone statue marked where the third glyphstone still stood. Shattered pieces of two others represented the stones in Bridgetower and Jabal

Tur that had already been destroyed.

The familiars raced up another flight of stairs, reaching yet another windowless room. A long reflecting pool with images of winged eyeballs carved into its walls stood at the center. The still water gave the otherwise dark room an eerie glow. Images rippling on the surface caught Aldwyn's eye, and he stepped forward to take a closer look. He saw that each image displayed a different snippet from the battlefield outside. Some showed the tree frogs of Daku valiantly fighting a skeletal elephant; others displayed Warden and his Turnbuckle disciples fending off the warthogs who had retreated from the fire caused by Anura's good luck; worst of all, Aldwyn could see Paksahara's zombie army closing in on the glyphstone. It would be only a short time before it was toppled.

Aldwyn glanced from one swirling image to the next. There was Orion, cut and bruised, but running swiftly regardless. Galleon and Banshee were faring better. Their combined magic was more than Lothar and his pack of wolverines could handle: all of them had been captured. A glimpse of his uncle Malvern's face looming. Urbaugh and his fighting force battling on despite casualties . . . Then Aldwyn did a double take—the picture of Malvern was so vivid. The eyes a ghostly white. The broken sword tip pierced through his rotting ear, glinting in the ever-changing light. The image kept getting bigger, larger than any of the other spyball visions. And why did Aldwyn smell rotting flesh? That's when he realized that the image of his uncle in the pool was not a vision, but a reflection. Malvern was directly behind him!

With no time to react, Aldwyn felt Malvern's claws dig into the back of his head, and his face was pushed down. He tried to grab a breath before going under but instead got a lungful of water. Aldwyn thrashed and struggled, but the force of his uncle's skeletal paw kept him submerged. Underwater, Aldwyn kept his eyes open, and the spyball visions all seemed to overlap, bleeding into one another. He could hear the strange, almost disembodied, voice of Malvern through the water.

You put up a good fight. Just like your mother did. The words filled Aldwyn with a rage greater

than any he had ever known. He continued to
flail, attempting to wrestle free from his undead
uncle's grasp, but to no avail. His eyes scanned
underwater for any object he might be able to lift
telekinetically and use to his advantage, but there
was nothing. His air supply was dwindling, but
rather than panicking, Aldwyn relaxed. His uncle
had taught him how to channel his innate talent,
and that it was not just solid objects that could
be moved. Aldwyn used his mind to push all of
the water to one side of the pool, away from him

and Malvern. Then he made it rise up like a tidal wave, knocking them back with the watery blast. Both cats slammed into the ground. Aldwyn hit chest first, and the impact from the stone floor shattered the three whisper shells that dangled from his necklace.

Malvern picked himself back up onto his feet and spit out a broken tooth. He looked down at the broken shells with a sneer. "Such a pity. The last reminders of your family gone."

Aldwyn coughed up the water he had swallowed and quickly filled his lungs with air. "I know where my sister is. We'll be reunited soon."

He charged toward Malvern and leaped paw first, pushing his uncle back. Malvern's skull cracked into the wall and he was left momentarily dazed.

Aldwyn glanced around and saw that his uncle was not alone. Two Maidenmere zombies had accompanied him. One was holding Gilbert facedown at the end of the pool, while the other was trying to drown Skylar. Malvern was still recovering from the shock of the blow. It gave Aldwyn a chance to help his companions. But who should he help first? The choice was easy, and not because he cared for one more than the other. No, it was easy because Gilbert had a lot more experience holding his breath underwater.

Aldwyn pounced at the skeletal cat holding Skylar down, tackling him to the floor and allowing the blue jay to come up for air. Then he telekinetically pulled the valor staff off Gilbert's back and clobbered the tree frog's attacker with it. And not a second too soon: Malvern was back on his feet, stalking toward Aldwyn.

"It's an amazing thing," said Malvern. "Once you're dead, you lose all fear. And once you do that, you become truly dangerous. Let me show you. And your friends."

He leaped forward, slashing at Aldwyn with his claws. As they struggled, Aldwyn furiously scratched at his uncle. He nicked the spike dangling from his ear and swatted at what was left of his face. Then he slipped out from under the zombie cat.

"There's a special place in the Tomorrowlife for traitors like you," said Aldwyn.

"Oh, I know. I've already been there and back.

That's why I plan on staying here a very long time."

"Well, don't get too comfortable," said Aldwyn.

His eyes narrowed, and he telekinetically tore the spike from Malvern's ear. Aldwyn brought it to his side and then shot it forward like an arrow, sending it hurtling right between his uncle's eyes. The metal spike cut through flesh and bone, killing Malvern for a second time. His bones fell limply to the ground.

"Neat trick," said Skylar, who was still catching her breath.

"Tricks are for circus monkeys," replied Aldwyn, echoing the very retort Skylar gave him when the two first met in Stone Runlet.

The two companions smiled at each other as together with Gilbert they raced up to the top floor of the Fortress. They reached the landing but instead of an open room they found the casting chamber sealed shut by a heavy iron door.

Aldwyn focused, and the tumblers inside the lock began to spin until they fell into place with a click. With a nod to Skylar, he pushed the door open.

Immediately the three familiars were met by

an energy blast that burned a hole in the wall behind them. Paksahara was already conjuring another attack, but by the time she unleashed it, the familiars were inside.

The three ducked behind a pedestal with a box full of black powder on top. Aldwyn took a moment to survey the surroundings. The casting chamber was a cold square room, colorless but for one exception: a floor-to-ceiling crystal urn holding different-colored wisps of magical essence within. There was a stone funnel whose tube bent into the wall; this was the mighty summoning horn through which all of Paksahara's dark magic was spread. A huge, wide-open window looked out onto the battlefield below, where the fight continued to rage on. The evil hare herself stood before a small spyball pool. She wore a carved wooden bracelet around her paw—the bracelet the woodpeckers had been tricked into carving to enable man to bring forth the Fortress on their own.

"Of all those in Vastia who tried to stop me, it was three animals who came closest," said Paksahara. "I would have expected nothing less.

We are, after all, superior to humans."

"That doesn't mean we should oppress those who are different from us," said Skylar. "And besides, whatever happened in the past is done. Humans today are not our enemies."

"Oh, you silly little bird," said Paksahara. "When will you learn that those on two legs will always keep you from what you desire most. Join me and I will give it to you. I'll help you bring back your sister from the Tomorrowlife."

At these words, the usually poised blue jay seemed momentarily disarmed.

"Yes, I have many friends in the Noctonati," continued the gray hare. "Animals who were present in the caves west of Mukrete. They told me everything about the questions you asked and your obsession with raising the dead. That's my specialty, you know. You could fly beside your sister once more. And she wouldn't be reborn as a zombie like the others. With time, we could learn to summon her whole. Flesh and blood."

Paksahara's words were clearly making a strong impression on Skylar.

"Don't let her tempt you," said Aldwyn. "I know

how much you've wanted this. But nothing is worth an alliance with *her*."

"She's my sister," said Skylar. "I'm the one who was responsible for her death."

"And it won't end there," said Paksahara. "All the libraries of Vastia will be open to you. Together we can unlock the secrets to every spell humans have ever known."

"What about the people that are still here?" Aldwyn urged Skylar. "What about Gilbert and me? Your mom and dad? Dalton?"

"Last chance, little bird," said Paksahara. "I won't ask again. Stand beside me or suffer the consequences."

Aldwyn had pleaded his case. Now it was up to Skylar. After a brief moment, she took Aldwyn's paw in one wing and Gilbert's webbed hand in the other.

"You're not going to get rid of me that easily," she said to her companions.

Just then a blast struck the pedestal, throwing the familiars off their feet and sending pieces of the pedestal and the box of black powder flying. Through the mist of obsidian now swirling in the air, Aldwyn watched as Paksahara transformed into an eight-foot-tall cave troll. Save for the pink glint in its eyes and the wooden bracelet encircling the tip of its giant finger, it would have been impossible to tell that this troll was indeed the gray hare. She swung her boulder-sized fists down at the three animals, narrowly missing them and leaving a large crater in the floor.

Gilbert reached into his flower bud backpack and removed some nightshade and juniper berries.

"I got this," he said.

"*Send a flame from whence you came!*" incanted Gilbert.

Aldwyn knew what Gilbert was attempting to do. Whenever the tree frog tried to conjure a flame fairy, the spell would accidentally self-destruct. He was hoping to use his poor spell-casting abilities to their advantage.

Just then a thumb-high flame fairy materialized, creating enough heat to warm Gilbert's toes.

"Hey, wait a second," said Gilbert. "That's what the spell is *supposed* to do. That doesn't make any sense."

"You sure picked a lousy time to get better at casting magic," said Skylar. Then she turned to Aldwyn. "Remember what Loranella said. The receiving vessel has to be destroyed to reverse the disenchantment. That crystal urn holds all human magic."

Aldwyn nodded and telekinetically lifted the fallen pieces of pedestal debris, launching them at the urn. But before they could make contact, Paksahara stomped forward and batted them away with her huge stone hand.

"Nuh-uh-uh," said the cave troll Paksahara.

Aldwyn sent a second barrage at her, but she shape-shifted again, changing from a cave troll into a day bat. She bared her fangs and soared above the flying rocks.

Aldwyn narrowly missed being scalped by the clawed foot from which the bracelet now dangled. Running past the casting tower's wide-open window, he suddenly stopped. A funnel of gray ash was rising into the sky: the third glyphstone had been destroyed.

The day bat hissed in triumph, and Paksahara's voice could be heard: "My Dead Army has done what most thought impossible. We have destroyed the three glyphstones once and for all!"

Then the bricks of the tower began to disappear. Within seconds, the walls surrounding them were gone.

"What's happening?" asked Gilbert.

"We're shifting," said Skylar.

The ceiling was now floating above them. Then the floor teleported. The next moment, Aldwyn, Skylar, and Gilbert were looking out at lightning snow. Paksahara had moved the Shifting Fortress to one of the three trident peaks of the Kailasa mountains.

The walls began to reassemble around the familiars once more, and the shift was complete. An icy breeze billowed in through the open casting chamber window, and at the same time Aldwyn felt something constrict around his leg. He looked down to see a frost python with pink, glistening eyes. Paksahara had transformed yet again, this time into a white-colored snake with fangs made of ice. As the creature tightened its grip on Aldwyn, Gilbert took out his valor staff and had the flame fairy light the wooden tip. He leaped on the python's nose and began jabbing at its teeth, melting the frozen incisors before they could bite down on Aldwyn. Paksahara was forced to release him from her grasp.

Outside the open window, the mountains disappeared, and in a flash the Fortress stood in the center of a jungle. The tip of the casting tower was high above the tree line, but Aldwyn could see below that the jungle itself was filled with flesh-eating plants. There were giant flower heads with rows of teeth lashing out at any passing creature.

Paksahara shape-shifted into one of the carnivorous plants and thrust a thorny tendril, striking at Skylar's wing. The force of the blow sent the blue jay straight out the open window. With one wing now injured, she struggled to keep herself in the air. The plant monsters waited hungrily for her on the jungle floor below. Skylar was moving herself back toward the window through sheer force of will when the Fortress began to shift again, the stone bricks of the tower rapidly disappearing.

"Skylar, hurry!" Aldwyn shouted as Skylar

desperately winged her way to the opening.

Gilbert bounced over to jab at Paksahara with his spear, while Aldwyn dashed to the window to reach out a paw to grab Skylar before she was left behind at this deadly location forever.

Just as the floor began to teleport away, Aldwyn pulled her back inside, and the tower made its next leap to the Aridifian Plains. When they turned around, they came face-to-face with Gilbert. And . . . Gilbert.

The tree frog's valor staff and Paksahara's wooden bracelet had both fallen to the ground. The two Gilberts looked identical, making it impossible to tell them apart. Even the pinks of the gray hare's eyes were undetectable.

"I'm Gilbert," said one of the tree frogs. "The other is a fake!"

"Don't believe her!" said the second. "I'm the real one."

It took Aldwyn only a moment to discover who his true companion was. He pointed at the second Gilbert.

"That's the imposter," he said. "That's Paksahara."

"How do you know?" asked Skylar.

"Because the real Gilbert has seven toes on his right foot."

Sure enough, there on the first Gilbert was a webbed foot with seven toes. The other tree frog had four toes on each foot. Paksahara wasted no time in tackling Gilbert and sending both of them tumbling back through the cloud of obsidian dust still floating in the casting chamber. When they emerged from the cloud, both Gilberts had seven toes and it was truly impossible to tell one from the other.

"Ow, that really hurt," moaned one of the Gilberts.

"What are you complaining about?" asked the other. "You're the one who tackled me!"

Aldwyn was studying the two tree frogs, and they really were identical. He didn't know what to do. Then he looked at Skylar and heard the blue jay speak.

Think, Skylar. There must be a way to tell them apart.

Aldwyn was confused. He could have sworn that her lips hadn't moved. He looked back at the two Gilberts. He turned to the first and heard Paksahara's voice.

Continue to play the fool. Sooner or later they'll come to suspect the real Gilbert as me.

Then Aldwyn looked to his right, at the other Gilbert. This time Gilbert's voice called out.

I really hope I live through this. I'd hate to miss my date with Anura. I can't believe she wants to hear my poetry. Wait. Stay focused, Gilbert!

What was going on? And suddenly, Aldwyn understood: he had inherited not only his father's talent of telekinesis but his mother's gift of telepathy, too. He could read minds!

It wasn't Grimslade's voice but his thoughts that Aldwyn had heard in the murky waters of the sewer market; then Simeon's before they left on their past walk; and finally Malvern's while his head was being thrust into the spyball pool.

"It's that one!" Aldwyn shouted to Skylar, pointing at the fake.

"How can you be sure?" asked the blue jay.

"Because I can read minds."

Paksahara knew she had been discovered. She conjured a ball of spikes and hurled it at Aldwyn, just missing his head.

"When the two of you suck in your final breaths, I want the last face you see to be that of your best friend," said the evil hare.

Aldwyn telekinetically lifted Gilbert's fallen valor staff and threw it at Paksahara, who was still in the guise of the tree frog. She jumped out of the way and raised her webbed hands, pushing the staff back at Aldwyn and striking him in the same leg where Malvern had bit him. An intense pain shot through his whole body.

Now Paksahara was narrowing her gaze on Skylar. But Aldwyn could see in her eyes that the blue jay had plans of her own. She flew several feet in the air and incanted: "*Astula Yajmada!*" With a mighty flap, Skylar touched her wing tips—one blue, one singed black—together, and a crimson spear materialized before shooting forward and impaling the imposter Gilbert straight through her chest. As Paksahara fell, she turned back into her true gray hare form, and then lay lifelessly on the ground.

Gilbert stumbled over, and Aldwyn limped, and the three familiars stood together over

Paksahara's dead body.

"I knew how to defeat her," said Skylar. "I had to cast Yajmada's Spear. It was your puddle viewing, Gilbert. It wasn't telling you that I was going to kill you. It was telling you that I was going to kill Paksahara. And it was showing me how to do it."

"Like I said, my visions never fail," said Gilbert. "What can I say? I'm good."

Aldwyn looked down at the gray hare who had hurt so many but now was finally gone.

"I can't believe it's over," said Aldwyn.

"It's not," replied Skylar. "Not until the wizards get their magic back." She flew over to the wooden bracelet and picked it up. "Take us back to Bronzhaven."

The Fortress began to shift at her command and moments later materialized in a spot not far from where it had been before, looking out at the battlefield.

"Aldwyn, would you like to do the honors?" asked Skylar.

Aldwyn focused on the largest chunk of pedestal debris still littering the floor and telekinetically flung it at the crystal urn. It made contact quickly and powerfully, leaving a gaping hole. With a green burst, all the trapped magical essences left the urn and swirled into the summoning horn.

The three familiars watched through the window as the magical smoke funneled out into the sky, snaking through the air and finding their wizards on the battlefield. The wisps wrapped around the humans and seemed to dissolve into their skin. The human warriors, who were crumbling under the overwhelming force of Paksahara's Dead Army, suddenly found their magic restored. A flurry of spells followed, and in just seconds, the tide turned. Skeletal beasts were evaporating into dust, and those that were not being struck down were retreating. The wolverines, dingoes, and goats sprinted away, choosing not to face humans casting fireballs and lightning bolts. Gundabeasts were being imprisoned with enchanted chains, while the remaining spyballs were shot down with messenger arrows.

"Now it's over," said Skylar.

The words had barely escaped her beak when

Aldwyn heard a clatter and groan behind them. He spun around to see Paksahara rising from the dead, straight out of the pile of black obsidian that her corpse had fallen on. No longer the fluffy gray hare she had once been, now she appeared like all the others in her Dead Army: flesh and fur left only in patches, bones sticking out everywhere. She was a zombie.

The three familiars charged her. Cat, bird, and frog struck a mighty blow in unison, sending the skeletal hare flying straight out the casting

chamber's open window. The zombie Paksahara grabbed hold of the sculpted stone lion's head protruding from the outer walls of the Shifting Fortress.

Aldwyn, Skylar, and Gilbert looked down at her through the opening.

"What are you going to do?" asked the dangling Paksahara. "Push me off? That wouldn't be very familiar-like of you."

"No," said Aldwyn. "We're not going to do anything. They are."

Paksahara turned to see what Aldwyn already had: a circle of bone vultures darting straight toward her. As the predatory birds tore into Paksahara's skeletal body, Aldwyn averted his gaze. He was left only to hear her screams as the bone vultures ripped her apart and flew away.

Peace had finally returned to the queendom.

Paksahara was dead.

19

A NEW VASTIA

"If I never drink a cup of radish cider again, it'll be too soon," said Jack.

Aldwyn let out a chuckle. It felt like weeks since he'd had a good laugh.

The familiar and his loyal were sitting in the courtyard of the New Palace of Bronzhaven. They were dipping their paws and feet in the small pond where the queen's golden eels swam in circles. It was their special spot, a place where all the pressures and worries of the world seemed far away. Jack was still recounting the anxious days he, Marianne, and Dalton had spent in the cellar at Stone Runlet. It hadn't been until their magic was suddenly restored that the three children ventured out from the safety of their subterranean hideaway and traveled back to Bronzhaven.

"And don't even get me started on pickled corn," continued Jack.

A week had passed since Paksahara's demise, and Aldwyn had slept for most of it. Although neveryawn nuts could keep one going without a full night's rest, there was nothing compared to curling up on a soft satin pillow, knowing Jack was nearby.

Aldwyn looked up to see magical torches once again hovering just above the castle walls. In fact, in the short time since the defeat of the Dead Army, Queen Loranella had recast her weather binding spells and reenergized the enchanted fences, and Vastia was well on its way to being returned to its former glory.

Dalton and Marianne stood across the way, looking at a wishing web. Although they tried to hide it, every so often Aldwyn caught glimpses of the two holding hands. Skylar and Gilbert were sitting on the other side of the pool. The tree frog was chewing up grubs, then spitting them out and putting them into his hand for Shady. The shadow pup happily lapped them up. Skylar was dictating to Scribius, who was copying every word she said into a diary. Since this whole adventure had ended, the blue jay had decided to write her memoirs. She said she'd been inspired by Kalstaff's many journals.

Aldwyn watched as Gilbert glanced into the water. He held up a webbed finger to Shady, who was noisily barking for more food.

"Shhh," said Gilbert. "Be quiet for a second."

He stared intently into the puddle, and when he looked up again, his face had gone pale.

"What is it?" asked Aldwyn.

"What is *what?*" asked Gilbert, playing dumb.

"I know that look," said Aldwyn. "What did you see?"

"Nothing," said the tree frog.

"Gilbert, what is it?" persisted Aldwyn.

But before he could press Gilbert further, Urbaugh and Warden approached from the palace.

"They're ready for you," said Warden.

The Prophesized Three and their loyals followed Loranella's advisors inside and down a long corridor. They passed the queen's library and the stairway that led down to the palace vault. Urbaugh and Warden stopped upon reaching the double doors that led into the grand hall.

"Is anybody else's tongue sweating?" asked Gilbert. The others just looked back at him blankly. "Okay, I guess it's just a frog thing."

Urbaugh opened the doors, and Aldwyn could see into the high-ceilinged hall. The room was grand, with stained-glass windows along the walls. The largest one was covered by a curtain. Colorful streamers floated in the air, and illusionary flowers blossomed and sprouted from the rafters, raining enchanted petals down on all those gathered. Every seat in every row was filled with humans and animals. Maidenmere cats, Daku tree frogs, and Nearhurst birds filled the front rows. Galleon stood with Delilah beside him. Behind them sat many of the seafaring folk from Split River; even some elvin pirates were among them. Unimice sat on human shoulders to get a better view. Mongooses and king cobras sat interspersed as well, having set aside, at least for the time being, their long-standing enmity.

At the front of the hall stood Queen Loranella, with a seven-pronged golden crown on her head. And standing right next to her was Galatea, leader of the lightmares, with an identical crown resting on hers. Stretching out on either side of them was a long, crescent-shaped table, with ten chairs to the left and ten to the right. Humans and animals sat in alternating seats. The people represented many regions of Vastia, while the animals gave voice to Vastia's countless species. Among them were Banshee, Navid, Marati, Anura, Gilbert's father, and Skylar's mother. Simeon would have been sitting there, too, Aldwyn thought, had he not passed into the Tomorrowlife. Even the raven's healing wings had been unable to undo the damage done by Lothar's claws. But Simeon had been at peace with his fate, eager to be reunited with his loyal, Tavaris.

Queen Loranella and Galatea bowed toward the Prophesized Three, and everybody else in the hall rose and did the same.

"To the newest heroes of Vastia," said Galatea.

"Here, here!" Shouts of approval rang out across the hall.

Aldwyn, Skylar, and Gilbert walked down the center aisle as hand, paw, scale, and wing reached out to touch the saviors. Jack, Dalton, and Marianne followed behind.

"You have not only saved us," said Loranella. "You have opened our eyes to a long-forgotten truth: whether you stand on two legs or four, we all stand together as one."

"Your legacy needs no monument," said Galatea. "It is collected before you now. We stand here as two queens rather than one."

"And for this, you will be honored," added Loranella.

She gestured to the large curtain that hung over the place where Paksahara had shattered the stained-glass window. A trio of birds flew up and pulled away the fabric, and the familiars looked up to see a picture in the glass that was a perfect replica of the bas-relief of Kalstaff, Loranella, and the Mountain Alchemist standing beneath three shooting stars twisting across the sky. Except this one celebrated Aldwyn, Skylar, and Gilbert in their place.

"You have fulfilled the prophecy," said Loranella. "Not because the stars foretold it. But because you believed in the greatness and courage within you and within each other."

Aldwyn looked at the image, and his chest swelled with pride. To think that an alley cat from Bridgetower had accomplished the impossible. With quite a bit of help from his friends, of course.

He looked at Skylar and Gilbert and smiled.

Then a ray of afternoon sunlight illuminated the stained-glass window, casting the grand hall in a blue, green, and black-and-white glow.

Aldwyn remembered the pale look on Gilbert's face after his latest puddle viewing. He leaned over and whispered in the tree frog's ear.

"Come on, Gilbert," he said. "What did you

see in that puddle viewing?"

"Not now, Aldwyn," said Gilbert. "Let's just say this isn't going to be our last adventure."

By the way Aldwyn's whiskers were beginning to tingle, he knew his friend was right.